Table of Contents

Voxx: Book One in the Mastered by the Zinn Alien Abduction Romance Series

By Alana Khan

Present Day
In Space Aboard the two-person vessel the *Drayant*

Day One

Victoria

I bolt out of deep sleep bombarded by a dozen things at once. My head is throbbing, it's so dark in here I can't see a thing, and I can't move. But overriding all the other input barraging my brain is the fact there's a vibrator on my clit.

I struggle to sit up but I'm locked down tight. I'm bound at my ankles and wrists. Fabric covers my eyes and binds my head to my bed. The only parts of my body I can wiggle are my hands and feet.

"Help!" My voice sounds hoarse, as if I've been screaming for hours. "Help!" Where am I? Was I roofied?

What's the last thing I remember? I came home after my last class, studied all night except for my one allotted program on Netflix—Season Two, Episode Six of Dexter—had hot cocoa, and went to bed. Did someone drug my cocoa? That doesn't even make sense.

I examine the facts that are in evidence: I am tied down, I'm blindfolded, my throat is raw, and a powerful vibrator is definitely nestled between my legs.

"Help!"

"There, there, Victoria. Calm yourself."

Victoria? Nobody calls me Victoria. His voice doesn't sound familiar. Oh my God, is this man going to kill me?

I read that telling a perpetrator about yourself might help. It makes you into a human being so they can't objectify and kill you.

"My name's Victoria, I like to be called Tori. I'm a second-year law student at the University of Iowa. I was born in Des Moines. My parents are still alive and will be very worried when I don't make my weekly phone call to them this morning. Look, I won't call the cops. Just let me go and—"

"Please calm yourself. I won't harm you."

"Won't harm me?" My voice isn't verging on hysterical, it *is* hysterical. "You've tied me up and you're raping me."

"This isn't rape. I have not entered your body."

Considering I'm the one in law school, this guy certainly knows how to stick to the letter of the law. Could he be one of my classmates? There's this older blond guy in my Corporate Law Class who I always catch staring at me.

"You're right. This would never be considered rape. And I don't think it qualifies as kidnapping since technically I haven't left my house. So if you just leave right now, you won't even go to jail.

"I'll give you a hint. Use alcohol or bleach to wipe down everything you've touched. That way even if I'm lying and call the police—which, trust me, I won't—they'll never get your prints. No harm. No foul. I'll just contact my parents—by the way, they're expecting my call any minute—and pretend like nothing happ—"

The stimulation to my clit jumps up a notch. No, it goes up ten notches, and an orgasm rushes at me with the speed and power of an 18-wheeler.

How could this be possible? Half the time when I'm with a guy and the mood music is playing in the background, and I've been plied with wine, and he's plucked my nipples just right and gone down on me for long minutes, I still have trouble coming. How is it I'm being held hostage by a mass murderer and my body's on fire?

The orgasm barrels down on me. It starts with quivering thighs and muscle spasms that ripple from pelvis to belly. I don't have a clue how to stop it. An explosion bombards my core and clit and boils down to the tips of my toes and roils up to the top of my head.

I scream a long, shuddering no-holds-barred, totally unladylike wail that burns my throat. Is this why my throat hurts? Was this not my first orgasm at the hands of this madman?

"That was your most powerful release yet, Victoria. I hope you enjoyed that." His voice is deep and sincere, which actually makes the situation even more insane.

"You're crazy. Let me go. Orgasms are like sneezes. Sometimes you can't stop them. That doesn't mean I'm enjoying them. Me, the person inside this objectified body, I don't like this. I don't like you, and you need to let me go."

Long, strong fingers stroke my head, sliding from scalp to the ends of my waist-length, chestnut hair. Tears snake down the sides of my temples. One thing is certain—this isn't a dream.

"Please turn that off," my voice doesn't sound strong and commanding anymore. I'm pleading. That's right, I'm begging my kidnapper to turn off the vibrator pulsing between my legs. The one that is ramping up my body even though I just had a mind-bending orgasm. Even though the last thing I want is carnal pleasure.

"What do you want from me?" I'm frantic.

"I want you to have one more release, Victoria. I want to give you one more spasm of pleasure."

"And then you'll leave? You'll let me go?"

"And then I'll turn off the vibrator."

As I lie here debating whether I want to give in to the orgasm that even now is building deep in my pelvis, my body takes on a mind of its own. He must have turned up the dial on the machine because my back is arching as far as possible against these restraints and my toes are curling. A category 5 hurricane blasts through my body in spasm after spasm of pulsing, quivering physical bliss.

I sag onto my bed. No, it's not my bed. It's firmer than a bed but softer than a table. It's angled so my head is up, and my ass is down, and my legs are splayed wider than at the gynecologist's.

Those long fingers comb through my hair, and warm gusts of his breath caress my face. He smells good. Do kidnappers/abductors/mass-murderers wear cologne for home invasions these days?

"You'll let me go now?" My lips are parched, and my throat aches from the scream that just ripped through it.

The vibrator stops and I take a deep breath.

"I promise I won't tell anyone. You were brilliant to blindfold me. You said you hadn't penetrated me, there will be no bodily fluids to test. You did everything right. Don't tell me your name, just clean up the crime scene, partially untie me, and be on your way. By the time I've worked my way out of these restraints—"

"Victoria, let me explain what's happening."

"No explanation necessary. The less you talk, the less I know. The less I know, the less I can tell the police. That is *if* I were to tell the police anything, because believe me, my lips are sealed."

"You're beautiful and so smart. I picked well when I chose you. If I had invaded your home and done this, your instructions would most likely keep me from being incarcerated. Brilliant. But since I'm not human, none of your coaching is necessary."

Oh my God. He's insane. Wasn't it the movie *Red Dragon* where the crazy guy killed people because he thought he wasn't human? Shit. That movie didn't work out well for anyone involved. I need to remind him of his humanity.

"Of course you're human," I hope my tone is warm and encouraging. "Things might have happened in your past that make you feel less than human, but we can overcome our traumas. They have really good forms of therapy these days. There's no stigma in needing help."

His chuckle, deep and rich, rolls over me. Fuck. He's not buying what I'm selling.

"You're very bright, Victoria. I can see your anxiety is rising. Let me explain what's happening. It will be a good way to begin our relationship."

Yeah, a far better way to begin than for me to wake up blindfolded with the world's most powerful vibrator dancing on my clit.

Oh, but he said the word relationship. A relationship implies another hour or day to live. Perhaps I can talk my way out of this. I'll listen to every word, every intonation. I'll find a crack in his armor and exploit it. I'm not giving up.

"I'm from planet Zinn. Similar to your Earth, my people poisoned our planet before we made necessary changes to protect it. It's beautiful now, healthy to live on, but due to the aftereffects of the heavy pollution, our race has all but stopped producing female offspring. Only ten percent of our children are female.

"Hundreds of years ago our government contacted yours. We showed them our scientific advances and our military capabilities. We made an Interstellar Compact so we could harvest a specific number of women each Earth year in exchange for military technology.

"Eligible Zinn males aged thirty to thirty-five are entered into a lottery each year. The lucky minority are allowed to choose a mate, bring her aboard their space vessel, and court her for fourteen days. At the end of the period—we call it the Quest—the female can choose to stay with the male or return to her home.

"We've developed techniques, with the help of your government, for you to return seamlessly to your old lives. All memory of our two weeks together will be wiped from your mind."

Holy shit. This is worse than I thought. He's totally looney tunes. How do I reason with batshit crazy?

"You know, Mr. Spaceman, if I get to decide whether to stay or go in two weeks, why don't you just save yourself some effort? You see, I have a life here on Earth. I'm sure you're nice and everything, but I'll never agree to go to your… planet with you. Just release me now, okay?"

"I'm Voxx."

"Pleased to meet you, Voxx. What a great story. You've got a wonderful imagination. Can you just let me go?"

"My people have been doing this for centuries and less than three percent of females return to Earth after two weeks with their male. I assume the ninety-seven percent who stay felt as you do right now. The agreement gives us fourteen days together. That is what we shall have." His voice is hard as iron.

I read about this when I studied case law pertaining to the criminally insane. He's got what they call a fixed delusional system. These beliefs can't be broken. I could ask him to look in the mirror right now and he'd say he sees a little green man. I could tell him our government would never do such a thing and he'd cite the Tuskegee experiment where the U.S. government injected its own healthy citizens with syphilis and left it untreated for decades.

I won't be able to convince him he's nuts. I'll have to figure out how to escape.

"Can I pee?"

"Certainly. Give us a moment to become better acquainted. I don't want to frighten you too badly when you see my form."

Riiiight. When I see him in his ever-so-special Zinnian form he'll have some reasonable explanation for why he looks like every other Earth male. Oh, and what about his English?

"So, Voxx, how is it you speak perfect English?" I can't wait to hear how he explains this.

"My mother is Earther. Actually, she's from Adel, Iowa. She tells me it's a small town outside of Des Moines. It's one thing about you that caught my interest as I searched for a possible mate on Earth social media."

Good job, Voxx. Clever. You didn't even need to invent imaginary high-tech subdural translators.

"You speak perfect English. Tell me something in Zinnish."

He talks gibberish for half a minute. I've got to hand it to him—he's inventive. Gibberish is hard to do. I tried it in drama class as an undergrad; it wasn't as easy as I thought. He imbued his nonsense with sentences and syntax. It could easily pass as a real language.

"What did you say?"

"It's a speech I've practiced since childhood when I dreamed of meeting my Earth mate. I will translate for you when you agree to call me Master and become my mate."

Call him Master? Become his mate? Fucking delusional.

"Are you ready to see my true form?"

"Can't wait."

I sense him stand from where he'd been sitting at my side. I picture him smoothing his soiled white wife-beater, or repositioning his balding mullet's comb-over. He efficiently unties, then unwraps my blindfold.

My eyes are still adjusting to the bright lights, yet I already see enough to curdle my blood. This isn't some psychopathic Bubba from the boonies, this is Voxx from Zinn—tall, muscled, and purple.

Voxx

I've spent my entire life preparing for this day. I learned English from birth; my mother ensured I was bilingual. I followed thousands of females' Facebook, Instagram, and Twitter accounts looking for matches. Then I hacked into Earth systems to find females' answers to those online personality tests they love to take.

As I narrowed my pool of applicants, I created and posted my own quizzes to find a compatible mate. Zinn males are dominant. We need females who can conform to our will. The point isn't to force or overpower our prospective mate, it's to allow her to blossom into her own femininity—to find the part of her that enjoys giving up her power to a male she cares for.

My society has thousands of books about finding the right prospect, and thousands more detailing every step to take during the precious fourteen-day window during which we have to meet, enthrall, and convince our mate to accept us.

The terrified expression on Victoria's face is not what I was hoping for. It's not just terror, I believe she's furious.

I stand a few feet from her and don't move, giving her time to get used to me. One reason we mate with Earthers is that their DNA does not overpower our own. I appear one hundred percent Zinn. I've spent my entire life looking at humans—my mother and aunts as well as Earth's primitive internet. She's seen no one other than her own species before.

"Your eyes are a lovely blue," I say, then smile. Zinn males don't smile often. My mother suggested I try not to do it around Victoria. She said it comes across as a grimace and makes me look less human, not more.

Victoria blinks and shakes her head.

"This is a dream, right? Right? Did someone put LSD in my cocoa?"

"No."

"Great bedside manner, Voxx. Work with me here. Let me hold out hope for a few more minutes."

"You're on my spaceship orbiting Earth. Article 3.2 of the Interstellar Compact states that we're not allowed to leave atmo until you're alert. Computer, begin programmed course." I offer her water and she drinks it in huge gulps, her eyes wide in fright looking off and to the left, avoiding me completely.

"I'll comply with your wishes to 'pee' in a moment. First, I want to ensure you understand the rules so you don't break them. I would hate to punish you so soon."

"Punish?" Her wan face blanches even paler.

"Your government allows us to discipline you as we see fit with the following exceptions: we must give you 1500 calories per day and provide you two liters of fluid every twelve Earth hours. Our punishments cannot leave any mark that lasts over forty-eight hours. We must allow you to sleep at least six hours per day.

"There's a long list of other rules. I will apprise you of them as it becomes necessary. I have devised additional rules which I'll review at dinner. Before I untie you, however, you need to know I will punish you if you try to escape, if you attempt to harm me, if you use any item to hit me, or if you touch any navigational or communication equipment. Repeat."

"What?"

"Repeat the rules. If I need to punish you I want there to be no excuse that you didn't understand the rules."

"What type of punishment are we talking about?"

"Here's a new rule—you need to respond to my questions with alacrity."

"Fuck."

"Here's another rule—you will not curse."

"No cursing? That's half my vocabulary."

"You've repeated that rule, now repeat the rest—with alacrity."

She considers for a moment, assesses me, then rattles off, "No escaping, no communicating, no navigating, no hitting."

"Good girl."

Until this moment, I didn't understand what the term 'rolls eyes' meant on Earth social media. I comprehend it perfectly now. "And no eye-rolling."

"No eye-rolling? That's an involuntary movement, like a muscle twitch or a sneeze. I have no control over it. Nor do I have control over saying fu—." She interrupts herself, closes her eyes, and breathes.

"Good girl. I'll let you go 'pee'." The restraint controls and all other ship functions link to an implanted chip in my brain. My species has found that it allows us to perform the training process more smoothly. After I release her, she sits up and rubs her wrists, then ankles.

"How long was I tied up?"

She stands then bends over, her hands on the small of her back, stretching. I'll have to remember I can't tie her down for so long in the future.

"Hours. I apologize. I didn't mean to hurt you."

She laughs. Well, it's more like a snort. No human I know has ever made that sound. I'm not sure what it means.

"What does that mean?" I thought speaking English all my life and perusing social media taught me everything I needed to know. I can't interpret this.

"What? I'm stretching."

"The animal noise that just escaped your mouth."

She looks bewildered.

"You made a noise when I said I didn't mean to hurt you. What did it mean?"

"Are you going to punish me for my answer?"

"Not unless it contains profanity."

"Do the Zinn understand sarcasm? Cynicism? You've abducted me, stripped me, restrained me to some kinky sex furniture, and forced me to orgasm without my consent. You inform me I'll be your fuckdoll—that's not profanity, that's a noun—for two weeks. And to top it off you haven't finished your list of what you'll punish me for and how you'll do it. And you have the gall…"

She's on a rant now. I don't think she could stop even if I threatened to punish her.

"You have the gall to say you didn't mean to hurt me? Irony!"

"I think you mean paradox."

I didn't mean to bait her, I swear, but when I see the whites all around her eyes, I realize I shouldn't have corrected her at that moment.

"Fuck you!"

She immediately realizes her error, covers her face with her hands and flinches away from me against the far wall.

"I'm sorry, Voxx. Dear God, don't kill me," her voice is a harsh whisper.

She squats on the floor to escape my wrath and begs again, "Don't kill me," as urine flows down her leg onto the floor.

In addition to taking females from Earth, we've also appropriated many of their dogs and bred them as domesticated pets. I've seen an anxious dog urinate on herself like that under extreme duress.

This is not proceeding as I had planned.

I gently grasp her wrist and escort her to the lavatory. After turning on the shower, I show her how to turn it off, hand her soap and washcloth, place a towel on the bar, and leave her a moment of privacy.

I hear her crying before I step away. As she would say, I fucked up. I imagined this day a thousand times in my mind. I read every manual. When I discussed my strategy with my mother, she agreed it was a sound one. She should know, shouldn't she? She's from Earth.

But nothing has worked as I'd planned. The numerous orgasms have not calmed her nervous system as the instruction manuals promised. Explaining the rules to her has not given her 'an enjoyable feeling of giving up control to a capable and masterful male.' And she didn't find my physical form pleasing as my mother suggested. Judging from her response to me, I believe I repulse her.

Victoria

Oh my God, this is a nightmare. Seriously, a huge part of my brain is still under the impression this is a dream. But out of all the unanswered questions this day brings, one thing is certain—it's real. I'm on a fucking spaceship that has launched into a journey into outer space with a purple alien who owns a flying dungeon of sex toys.

Yeah, I saw his little sex arsenal somewhere between catching my first glimpse of his purple face and pissing all over myself on his floor. First, there was the sex furniture that was a hybrid between a pommel horse and a St. Andrew's cross. Then there was a neat stockpile of whips, dildos, butt plugs, and other stuff I couldn't catalog fast enough.

Mr. Perfect appears to be a dungeon master yet doesn't want me to cuss. And when I'm done with this shower, I'm getting punished. My anger disappears, replaced by mind-numbing dread. He said he could punish me any way he wanted as long as it didn't leave a permanent mark. I guess cutting off a limb is verboten, but whipping with a cane is perfectly acceptable. I'm terrified.

"Victoria. Water is scarce on a space vessel. You have less than a minute before the program turns off your shower," he calls through the metal door. As soon as I rinse off, the water stops. I'm not surprised. As surreal as this experience is, he hasn't said one word that isn't true.

I dry off and sit on the toilet trying to devise a plan of action. The engine's thrum vibrates under my feet. I peeked out the bridge windows earlier; we're really out in space. There's no escape. I'm locked in this tiny vessel with a psychopathic madman. There's no way out of this.

"Victoria. You can't stay in there. You need to come out within one minute to receive your discipline. If you're not out by then, I'll have to increase the punishment."

With the thick, white towel wrapped around me, I step out, eyes downcast. I'm afraid I'll accidentally roll my eyes, inadvertently drop an F-bomb, or incite his wrath in a thousand other ways. My hands are shaking. I'm a wuss. I hate pain.

"Sit." He points to a small, hard metal chair in the corner of the bedroom.

The guy is huge. By my guess, he's way over six feet. He's wearing black boots and cargo pants. No shirt. He's built big. Muscles from head to toe. All of them are purple.

I'm sitting, inspecting the metal floor, waiting to be hit. I glance at the neat wall of torture devices in the adjoining room, wondering which one he'll use on me. And for how long.

"I want to apologize. You asked to relieve yourself and I didn't comply with your wish. Your… episode was avoidable and completely my fault. That being said, I owe you a punishment. Do you recall what it is for?"

"I cursed." *Please Tori, I beg myself. Don't provoke him further. Be contrite, and maybe he'll go easy on you.*

"Not only did you curse, you cursed directly at me. Must I tell you that merits more punishment?"

I stifle a groan. *Shut up. Don't say a word.*

"I'm sorry," I'm not certain I managed to sound repentant.

"For cursing, the humiliation of urinating on yourself is punishment enough. You will also need to clean up the mess immediately. You will not wear clothes for the remainder of your sojourn with me. That includes your towel."

He waits, looking pointedly at the towel wrapped around me. I stand and remove it, keeping it grasped between thumb and forefinger, not knowing what to do with it.

"Get on your hands and knees. Use the towel to absorb the liquid, then you may clean it with this."

I follow him out of the bedroom and he shows me a liquid cleaning product and something I assume is like a space-age ShamWow. I clean 'with alacrity'. I'm a quick study, realizing life will be easier if I keep the big, purple asshole happy.

"Good girl," he says after I've placed the gross towel in the laundry machine, my task complete. I realize I performed that assignment in the nude and I'm standing here like a Playboy bunny, sans puffy tail and pointy ears.

"Your punishment for cursing directly at me needs to be more… personal. You will remove my clothes with care, fold them neatly, and place them on that chair." He indicates with a nod of his head. "You will kneel before me while I recite the remainder of the rules."

When I don't move fast enough, he adds, "I'll start with the first rule now, Victoria. When I give you an order you will say, 'yes, Sir'. And do I need to explain what the word 'alacrity' means?"

"No, Sir."

I'm running on impulse now. The Victoria of ten hours ago would have kneed any motherfucker audacious enough to say or do half the shit Voxx has. I would have picked up that chair and bashed him over his thick skull—repeatedly—until his brains were splattered all over the room.

The Victoria of right this minute? The one in a spaceship? With a purple alien the size of a house standing with his hands on his trim hips waiting for her to jump at his order? She can't hurry over to him fast enough to kneel and pull off his fucking pants.

I fumble at his waistband, trying to figure out the alien fastener. I just want to get the job done.

"We'll begin at the beginning, shall we?"

I'm waiting for him to take matters into his own hands and remove his pants. Instead, he lifts my hands and shows me how to unclasp the waistband. He re-clasps it, then says, "Everything I request of you is in service to our bond, Victoria. To that end, all intimate tasks, no matter what I request, no matter how small, need not be accomplished in haste. Imagine I'm a lover. A male you wish to please, you wish to excite. Your every step, every action, should endeavor to entice me. Go back to where you were standing."

I hurry back to the area where I peed. The shiny metal floor is now clean and dry.

"Look at me like you're seeing me for the first time. As if I'm the most handsome male in the ballroom of a huge party. As if you've been stealing glances at me all night and now I've beckoned you over."

While I'm still ordering my gaze to lift from the floor, he whispers, "with alacrity," as if he's coaching a forgetful actor from the sidelines.

I look over at him, then drink him in from glossy black boots up muscular calves and thighs, trim waist, ripped abs, and thick, corded neck. The glowing geometric tattoo on his upper left arm catches my attention, then I study his face for the first time since we met.

Magenta lips, aquiline nose, almond-shaped eyes with silver irises, and long, white hair. If I didn't hate his guts, I'd think he was handsome.

I can imagine what he described, glimpsing him at a party and following him with my glance all night. I'd be attracted to that face, that body, in a heartbeat if I didn't know he was a sadistic, controlling prick.

"Walk toward me as if you want my eyes on you, Victoria. As if you want my cock to harden at the way your hips sway. You're a female who knows you can command a male's attention by moving your lips into a practiced pout, or by looking at him as if you're wondering what his cock will feel like in the warmth of your mouth."

His words hang in the air as if they are things I can touch, not just thoughts. I'm afraid to look at him because those ideas are now planted in my brain, and I do wonder what he'll taste like. I hate myself for it.

I walk toward him, half nervous teen, half seductive woman.

"Good job, Victoria. Go back and do it again. You can do better." Gone is any hint of domineering command from his voice, now his words are all deep, mellifluous seduction.

And God help me, I do it. I walk back to my starting point, then stalk toward him as if he's Bradley Cooper and Jason Momoa rolled into one. I look him up and down and try to convince myself I'm doing this because he ordered it and not because I'm loving the admiration in his eyes. The look that says he's getting harder with every step I take.

"That's right. What a good girl you are," he says, his voice husky. "Slide onto your knees and slip open my pants. Nice and slow, as if you're unwrapping a package."

Oh yeah, unwrapping his package. I tell myself he's drugged me with an aphrodisiac. I'd never be so obedient on my own. I'd never cave in to a purple asshole's demands with just the threat of violence, would I? No, not without some type of compliance drug.

His pants are around his ankles now, and he steps out of them with power and agility.

"Lean back on your heels and take stock. We'll be getting to know each other much more intimately during the Quest."

I lean back as commanded, reminding myself how much I hate him even as I admire what I see. 'Well-endowed' doesn't do it justice. 'Magnificent', 'proud', and 'impressive' come to mind. It's thick and long and purple, a deeper shade than the rest of his skin. It's pointed at the ceiling, with a glistening bead of liquid pearling at the tip.

He steps toward me, breaching the few inches between us. I wondered for a moment if he would thrust himself in my mouth without my permission, but his sole purpose in moving was to pet my head. His sweet touch changes everything.

I forget my hatred for a moment and breathe deep for the first time today. My exhale releases slow and easy. My shoulders relax.

"That's right, Victoria, I don't wish to harm you. I don't want to hurt or punish you. I want this."

Both hands are stroking my hair so sweetly I could drown in it. Is it because I thought I was inches from death earlier today and now I'm so fucking happy to be alive I'd accept anything? I don't know. I allow his touch to calm me. The moment seems to stretch into eternity.

There's a tiny part of me that's mesmerized by his bobbing purple cock. It's perfectly shaped, and the drop of lavender liquid on its tip beckons me.

Nope. Whatever drug he's pumped into the water won't work on Victoria Franklin.

I want to get up, but fear it will merit another punishment. I await further orders.

"Let's review the rules and then you can go to bed."

I glance around and notice the sex apparatus taking up a big part of the combination bridge and galley. The only separate area on this small vessel is the bedroom attached to the bathroom where he allowed me to take a shower.

"You will call me Sir at all times until you choose to stay with me, then you will call me Master in private."

Fat chance. I stifle a smirk.

"You will follow all orders with a positive attitude."

Even when I'm hating you, are you kidding?

"We will begin your sexual training tomorrow. I will not allow you to have sexual release until given permission."

Sexual training? I glance at the neat array of sex toys and implements of torture—my stomach drops to the floor. I don't like pain.

"Victoria?"

Crap, he's waiting for my response. Did I miss something?

"I'm sorry, Sir?"

"That's the complete list of rules I need to share at this moment. Now it is your turn to say 'yes, Sir'."

"Yes, Sir."

"Here are your 1500 calories for today." He holds out three nutrition bars.

"Thank you, Sir."

He hands them to me, smiling and nodding. "Good girl."

Five minutes later he's showered and we're both in bed.

"I want you to watch this."

There's a one-foot by two-foot screen on the wall.

"Oh, Netflix and chill?" I ask, assuming he'll have no idea what I'm talking about.

"No, I'm afraid."

"Are you familiar with every pop culture reference on Earth?"

"I've spent a lot of time on Earth Facebook."

Yeah, stalking women. I control a shiver. It is disturbing and creepy knowing he's familiar with every post, picture, and emoji I've ever shared.

"Are you trying to titillate me with alien porn?" I snark.

"I doubt you will find this arousing. Let me know if you do. I can arrange similar vids for your edification and amusement in the future."

The video comes to life and I see a montage of human after human breaking rules on various Zinnian ships. One woman sneaks out of bed to use the comm on the bridge, one starts a fire in the galley, one picks up a chair and hits her male, he just shakes his head and grabs her wrist.

On and on the vid shows every manner of escape attempts and efforts to attack the male. None succeed. Then the vid scrolls through various punishments each girl receives in response.

Spliced in at the end of the reel is a picture of Voxx, apparently at home on Zinn. The sky is purple. How quaint, everything is color-coordinated. He picks up a metal rod as thick as my wrist and slams it against the ground. It thuds, but doesn't bend. Then he grabs the bar and pulls the ends together almost without effort. It leaves no doubt in this viewer's mind that he's a million times stronger than me. The subtext isn't at all subtle—don't fuck with him. Point taken.

The video shuts off.

"I did not follow through with your punishment earlier today because I wanted us to get off on the right foot. I will never hesitate to punish you in the future. Do you understand?"

"Yes, Sir."

"Good girl."

Voxx

"You saw what I did to the bar on the vid. Tell me you understand I won't allow you to do anything in this bed to harm me."

"Yes, Sir."

"No pillow on my face, no choking me with your hands or a sheet. I'm bigger and stronger and will retaliate with one hundred times more force than you're capable of. Do you understand?"

"Yes, Sir."

"I don't want you sneaking out of bed when I'm asleep. I've keyed every system on this ship to my biometrics; you can't access any of our technology."

"Yes, Sir."

"I want you to stay in bed so I can sleep soundly. I'm putting this collar on you. It will sound an alarm if you break the rule."

I pull out the thick leather training collar that's programmed to alarm should she leave the bed. "Sit." She sits up immediately, pleasing me immensely. "Good girl." I snap it on.

She lies back down, as far from me as possible. Her breathing becomes labored and irregular. A moment later, she sits up. When I turn on the lights, she's pulling at the collar, her eyes wide in fright. She's scratching red lines into her neck, trying to yank it off.

"Help!" she rasps. "Can't…"

Grabbing her hands, I tear them from her throat.

"Can't. No."

These aren't histrionics. She's so terrified she can't stop herself. I press my finger to the biometric lock and the collar falls open. She rips it off her throat, gasping for air.

"Can I… Sir?"

I have no idea what she wants, but tell her, "Yes."

After jumping out of bed, she paces the little room, around the bed one way and then back. All the while she's massaging her throat and gulping for breath. Then she winds down, slowing her step, breathing more regularly but still panting.

"Whoa, that took me by surprise," she says. "I've never had one of those before."

"One of what?"

"I'm no doctor, but I'd say that had to be a panic attack. Fuck, that was no picnic."

Her eyes round in her face and she flinches, waiting for punishment for her profanity.

"We'll start with three judicious uses of that word each day without punishment," I offer generously.

"Good, 'cause I don't think I can go cold turkey." She settles onto the bed, purposefully breathing slow and steady. "Give me five minutes, Voxx, I mean Sir. Please? Five minutes before you put that back on me?"

"Yes, certainly. I could give you release. To help you calm down?"

"You think I need to come right now? Seriously?"

"The manuals state that orgasms relieve human females of many anxieties and ailments. They seem very powerful. I imagine it would take your mind off your pressures."

"You think a big, purple alien assaulting me with vibrators would take my mind off my pressures? You need more Facebook time."

"There are many memes suggesting that sex cures everything. Did I misunderstand?"

She breathes deeply and scoots her ass toward me. "You can try the collar again. I think I can handle it. The anxiety just struck me out of the blue."

"Lie down, Victoria. I'll wait until you're asleep to put the collar on."

She lies as far from me as possible, her knees hanging off the bed. I throw my arm over her and slide her toward me, my front to her back.

"You belong to me now, Victoria. For the next thirteen days, you're mine. I will get to know every crevice of your body and how to take it to the heights of pleasure. I also want to know your mind."

Pictures of the females' faces in the vid we just watched bombard me. I don't want that. I don't want her to look at me with fear and dread. I want her to look at me the way she did earlier when she was in her full feminine power, walking toward me with her hips swinging.

"Then how about a new rule, Sir?"

"I make the rules, Victoria," my voice is stern; she has to understand I'm in complete control.

"I know. How about you make a rule that every night we have ten minutes where you're Voxx and I'm Tori? How about during that time I can cuss without retribution? How about for those ten minutes I get to speak my real mind? I'll call you Sir and follow your orders all day. For that little slice of time, ten measly minutes, six-hundred seconds, you can get to know the real me."

Very few things frighten me. I've completed two years of mandatory military service. I oversee complex, costly projects at my job as an architect. Yet my stomach clenches at the thought of little Victoria telling me her truth. I don't think I'll like what she has to say.

"Yes, on one condition. If you act as if you enjoy my touch all day during training tomorrow, I will give you your ten minutes of truth."

I tell myself I made the deal to help her. It will be so much easier for her if she doesn't fight the process. But in my heart, I admit I want her to enjoy my touch.

Keeping one arm around her feminine waist, I stroke her hair with the other. Maybe it's my imagination, but I believe my touch calms her.

After she falls into a fitful sleep, I reflect for hours, replaying every moment since she awoke on this ship. I need to reevaluate the playbooks. I don't care how many elders or for how many centuries common wisdom dictated the use of force to get a female to comply. That was a terrible strategy.

I chose Victoria. I want her and I want her to desire me. This female won't agree to be my mate if I stick to the old tactics. I've already made too many mistakes.

Now that I've met her, I can't imagine how she'll forgive or forget waking up tied down and blindfolded. The forced orgasms? She was so terrified she pissed down her leg.

She'll have a hard time putting that behind her.

I'll forge new ground and trust my own instincts. I'll emerge from these two weeks with a mate who loves me and wants to submit to me. And I'll do it on my own terms.

Day Two

Victoria

That wonderful moment between being fully asleep and mostly awake where you're not sure where you are? That moment went way too fast. I barely get five seconds of believing I'm back on Earth in my own sheets before I remember I'm on an alien ship.

The scent coming from the galley not ten feet away smells like nothing on Earth.

"Come, eat," Voxx calls as if I'm his girlfriend and he's cooking breakfast before we hurry off to a day at the office. But I'm his sex slave and we'll be forced together in the confines of this ship for the next thirteen days.

Why did I agree to pretend to enjoy his touch all day just so I can tell him off every night? He'll do whatever perverted shit he chooses. At least this way I get to tell him to go fuck himself for ten blissful minutes.

I glance around for clothes for about half a second before I remember the no-clothes rule.

"Food's ready," he sounds impatient.

"Coming. Just putting on my clothes." Maybe Mr. Stick-Up-His-Ass will develop a sense of humor over the next two weeks.

He motions for me to sit on one of the two stools tucked under the tiny metal eating bar in the galley. Weird, cold, and unsanitary are the thoughts floating through my head as my naked ass plops onto the metal stool.

The ship is small, maybe twenty by twenty-five. Every surface is either metal or a computer screen, except for the large windows at the front of the ship. It's black out there, and I realize for the first time it's always dark in space unless you're flying into a sun.

There's a bridge with two large squarish chairs facing the windows. The bridge connects to the combo galley/sex room, which connects to the bath/bed en suite. It's your typical no-frills, standard-issue sci-fi space vessel.

My eyes skitter from the wall of pain, where he stores his sex toys, to his face as he eases onto the stool next to me, one full plate in his hand. Oh well, at least the alien Geneva Convention mandates food every day for us prisoners of war. I guess I get to watch now and eat later.

"Put your feet on the top rung of your stool," he orders. When I comply, one corner of his mouth lifts in just the hint of a smile as he feeds me a forkful. "Does that please your Earther palate? If not, I can provide something else."

"Fine," I snip even as my taste buds sing at the delicious melding of flavors.

"Open your knees."

I spread my legs an inch and stare at him. I'm vibrating with anger and if looks could kill he'd be incinerated. He doesn't have to be psychic to read the depth of my hatred. He attentively feeds me another bite of food as if we're on an intimate date.

"Wider."

I'm paralyzed. I'm too afraid to say no, but I can't order my body to comply.

"Wider," he's using his drill-sergeant voice.

My eyes round in fright because as much as I don't want to be punished, I can't make myself do it.

"I don't want to." I don't know how those words escaped my mouth. This guy could kill me with one well-aimed backhand. Too late, I cover my mouth with my hand and hunch down to avoid possible punishment.

He stands and hulks over me, then leans within an inch of my face.

"I'm in charge on this vessel, Victoria."

"Yes, Sir." Cowering, my gaze is glued to the floor. I've never been this terrified.

He moves to my right, giving me a full view of the wall of pain.

"I don't want to harm you with any of those." Despite the fact that he's towering over me, his voice is warm and sincere, almost as if he's rooting for me to do the right thing to avoid punishment.

He lets the words hang in the air for long moments as I catalog every whip and leather binding.

"You decide how much you don't want to comply with my directions, versus how much you don't want to be introduced to any of the implements on the wall." He runs his hand through his hair in impatience, but otherwise doesn't move a muscle. I'm don't know if he's ready to backhand me or feed me more food.

What do you know? His pep talk motivated my knees to separate. And even more disconcerting? My body's responding in an unexpected way.

Why is this turning me on? I open my legs wider and receive another bite of food along with a "Good girl." My arousal makes me hate myself. Full-on self-loathing.

He reaches over and removes the thick, leather collar. I'd forgotten it was there, which is great because that panic attack last night sucked.

He drags his stool to the perfect viewing position, sits down, then eyes me while he eats. With every mouthful, he looks like he'd rather be snacking on what's between my thighs. His plate's half full when he stands, hands it to me, and says, "Have as much as you want."

His back is to me as he neatens the kitchen. "Today we get to explore what's mine."

"Yes, Sir." Crap! I'm experiencing equal parts loathing and arousal. How is that even possible?

He folds his arms in front of him and inspects me. I take this moment to give him the once-over. He's human-looking. Except for the purple skin. Well, except for the purple skin and the way he's built. I mean, I've seen men built like this on Earth, but there's only a hundred of them and they all compete in the Mr. Universe contest. And the cock. I haven't seen that many cocks up close and personal. But the ones I've seen, and the ones on the free porn sites online, they're not this big.

I glance up and see he caught me looking. Tough.

"Like what you see?"

"I'm trying to figure out how to tolerate it," I snip. He thinks I'm going to adore him? Give him compliments? I didn't receive the memo.

"Cup your breasts," he orders.

After placing one boob in each palm, I await further instructions.

"Remember last night when I described being at a ball? Imagine the male of your dreams escorts you onto the private balcony outside the ballroom. You have on a low-cut ball gown. You want to reveal yourself to him, to encourage his interest. How would you present yourself to this male?"

Lifting them a bit higher, I stifle my urge to tell him 'this is all I got, there ain't no more'.

"I'll be back," he tosses over his shoulder as he stalks into a cubby off the bridge.

'I'll be back'? Is he doing a bad Terminator impression? That seems fitting.

Ten minutes later, he returns with a robin egg blue ball gown. It's like something out of *Gone with the Wind*—frilly sleeves, bell-shaped skirt, and a low, scooped neckline.

"Put this on."

I'd never in a million years admit it, but I've always wanted to wear one of these. I shimmy into it and swish first one way and then another, loving the way the satin slides over my naked flesh.

"Scarlett O'Hara's dress needs petticoats," I grouse.

"Maybe later."

"Now, how would you present those beautiful breasts to the male you've been admiring for hours?"

I'm running a hundred different conversations with him in my head, each more bitchy and petulant than the last. What I say is nothing.

I peg him with a sexy stare and swipe my finger back-and-forth half an inch under my neckline. When I have his full attention—and that's easy to figure because he's naked and his huge cock is standing hard and bobbing at me—I reach in, cup my right breast, and lodge it on top of the material.

"Very good. Now the other." His mouth is dry, and for once he's not so full of cocky swagger.

"Yes, sir." While I'm repeating the action with my left boob, I allow myself to enjoy this moment. I'm captivating him. I have a feeling this will be the only good minute of the day, maybe the week. I must say, it's enjoyable to have the power to shut him up with my not-so-abundant charms.

"Your breasts are perfect," his tone is husky.

He waits a moment more. I wonder if he's waiting for me to thank him—in your dreams asshole—or if he's still drinking in my gorgeousness. I have to remind myself he's only seen a few women in real life, and all of those were probably his mother's generation. If he wants to act as if I'm the prettiest thing he's ever seen—and he's doing a great job of it—so be it.

"Show me how you like them stimulated."

He pulls up a stool and sits a foot away. I half expect him to pull out a notepad and don a pair of horn-rimmed glasses.

He looks me square in the eye. "Are you refusing an order?" His tone isn't playful. And the word 'order' has taken our little exchange from comedy to drama.

"Yes, Sir." When he glowers, I backtrack. "No, Sir. I am complying. With alacrity."

I'm not exactly certain how to excite myself upon command. Perhaps my arousal isn't part of the equation—only his.

I roll, then pluck first one nipple then the other. "That's it." I shrug.

"Don't lie."

"That's how it's done."

"If that's how it's done, why aren't you aroused?"

"I… thought I was giving a tutorial. I didn't realize I was supposed to turn myself on."

The lights dim. I'm not sure how he does it, I wonder if somehow the ship connects to his nervous system. Is he a cyborg or something?

"Breathe in." He waits for me to comply. "That's right, now breathe out. Pretend you're in bed late at night in the dark and you're thinking of a male you're interested in. As you imagine him pleasuring your breasts, what do you picture? Let your fingers be his, Victoria."

I pluck until they're hard, then twist and pinch them gently. Popping my eyes open from half-mast, I look over to notice he's inched over to observe a close-up of the action.

"Keep doing that, Victoria. I'm waiting until the smell of your arousal perfumes the room."

"Yes, Sir." I want to sound petulant with a touch of fuck you, but I come across as breathless and pre-occupied.

I get back to work, my eyes closed, and realize he's moved even closer. His breath whispers across the back of one hand. I want to hate everything about this moment, but I can't.

I smell the spicy scent of him, a lock of his hair brushes the back of my hand, his huge, masculine presence is so close I can't ignore it—and I don't want to. The last thing I want is for the scent of my arousal to perfume the fucking room, but this is intimate and exciting and every single nerve ending is on fire.

Dragging my nails across the tip of each nipple pulls a little sigh from me.

"Victoria likes that? Do it again," his voice is so deep it's like a depth charge rumbles through my body.

Why is being his little fuckdoll so stimulating? I'm dripping wet, probably making a spot on Scarlett O'Hara's fancy blue dress.

"Yes, Sir." I scrape my nipples again, making my core pulse in need.

"Do it again, harder."

I do. Instead of it hurting as I'd expected, it makes me clench my thighs.

"Your Sir will relieve you, Victoria. I will bend my head to your breast and scrape it with my teeth until you moan. Or I could slide my hand from here..."

He slips off his stool, squats at my feet, and caresses my ankles up my calves to my knees. He's poised there, thumbs on my inner knees, waiting for me to give the word.

"I could slide up from here and touch your wet slit. I could put the fire out." His thumbs make lazy figure eights where they're resting only one foot from my core.

"You don't even have to ask. Reach out and touch my hair and I will lavish attention on your exquisite breasts. Touch my shoulder and my hands will quench your fire. In the meantime, don't stop what you're doing," his voice is silken, persuasive; he makes it sound so easy to comply, to let him take me to the heights of pleasure, give me release.

This is insanity. I'm a kidnapped sex slave with a handsome purple male at my feet. He wants to make me feel good, and for some insane reason scales are tipping toward saying yes. I press my thighs together to quench my own damn fire, then I ruminate on horror films.

Jeepers Creepers, my personal favorite. Low budget and scary as fuck. But what I really need to douse my desire are vastly more horrible pictures.

I bring out the big guns: *Hellraiser*. I replay every awful scene of the movie while I keep tweaking my nipples. *Take that, Purple Asshole*. My arousal will never perfume this room.

Five minutes later he unbends and stands over me. Fuck he's tall. He's got to be mad that his little offer to douse my fire failed. I wait for him to backhand me, or call me over to the sex furniture to shove something in me or whip my ass. He does none of that.

"Please disrobe and fold the dress over the first mate's chair." He points to one of only two padded seats in the vessel. "You may have one hour respite. Let me show you how to use the vid player and the reader."

As much as I hate him, I have to admit he's used a great deal of self-restraint since we met. If what he says is true, he's never been this close to a female his age, much less had sex with one. We laid naked in bed last night, his cock pulsing against the small of my back without reprieve, yet he never stepped over a boundary. I think this whole fourteen-day exercise is about more than just sex. He wants me to like him. That's ridiculous, I'll never let that happen.

The vid player he provided has nothing on it but human/Zinn porn. Ditto the e-reader. Big guy thought of everything. Keep me bored or plied with sexually stimulating material. When I get back to Earth, I might never want to look at a male, I mean man, again.

"Sir, when do my fourteen days expire?" I ask pointedly while looking at the clock on the wall. When he tells me, I do the math then inform him, "By my calculations, I have 320 hours to go. Do you have paper and a pen? I can make a scratch-off like an Advent calendar."

I'm pretty sassy for a girl living with a guy who brought twenty-two female hitty things with him into space. Although I've never been into S&M, I think there are canes, paddles, whips, and some other things I have no interest in exploring.

I also cataloged four butt plugs of varying sizes and ten vibrators, some of which are for external, and some for internal use. These seem to be of human design. I wonder if he produced them magically like he did Scarlett's dress.

"You seem very interested in the toys. Pick one."

Shit. "Just looking, Sir."

"Pick one. We'll play when your rest period is over." There's steel in his tone.

Damn, I think curiosity really did kill the fucking cat.

"Say 'yes, Sir' and pick one immediately or I will do the picking."

"Yes, Sir," I say as I grab the smallest thing I see, it's not much bigger than a matchbook.

~.~

"Rest time is over." He rises from his captain's chair and stalks over to me. "What did you pick?"

I hold it up in my palm.

"Do you know what that is?"

"No." I inspect it now and realize before he tells me.

"It's a nipple clamp. You'll need two." He searches for its mate and holds them both in his palm. "Why did you pick these?"

"They were the smallest things I saw."

"As you must have assumed, I've never been with a female before. I'm prepared though, Victoria. I've watched many Earth vids. We can explore these together. I must say I'm surprised. I assumed you would pick something to administer pleasure, not pain."

"Can I have a do-over?"

He cocks an eyebrow.

"A re-do? Can I pick something different?" I spot the little silver bullet vibe on the bottom shelf. I should have picked that. I'm an idiot.

"You've informed me we have 319 hours, we'll have time to explore all the toys."

"Remind me why we're doing this again? You know I'll never stay with you. Please let me go."

"Here's a new rule. I'll let you ask to leave once per day. Any more than that will result in punishment. You've had your one for the day. Might I remind you how to address me? You've forgotten the rules already." The corners of his mouth turn down in disappointment.

"No, Sir. I haven't forgotten the rules. I guess I didn't realize my rest period was over."

"Rest period or not, the rules are the rules."

"Yes, Sir."

"You asked me to remind you why we're doing this. We're bonding."

I snort. Shit, he hates when I do that.

"Your idea that we talk freely ten minutes each evening is a good one. I want you to reserve all eye rolls, snorts, and negative comments for those ten minutes. Trust me, you're the only female captive who's ever been given this opportunity. I would cherish it if I were you."

"And cherish it I will, Sir," I manage to say without a whiff of sarcasm.

"Good girl. Stand on the red square."

There's a red square painted between the sex table and the kitchen. I'd wondered what it was for. I guess I'm about to find out.

"You're to stay in this square. You may not leave it until I give you permission. Put your hands behind your back."

I hold my wrists behind my waist. I'm already not liking this. He's glaring at me. Oh yeah. "Yes, Sir."

He nods, satisfied.

He examines my breasts. First, he hefts them as if deciding what they weigh. Then he glides his thumbs over the nipples. The traitors stand right up and say hello to him. He slips behind me and plays with them exactly as I did prior to my rest break. He tugs, then twists, then scrapes them with his thumbnail.

I gasp sharply. Why does that have to feel so good? My clit is already quivering. In a minute I'll be dripping wet.

He bends, his mouth at my ear, "You like this Victoria." If his husky, breathy tone wasn't clear enough, his cock pulsing against my back is a giveaway that he likes it, too.

"Open your legs. I want to smell you."

"Yes, Sir." I do as I'm told and have no doubt he can smell me—I sure can.

He moves in front of me, lifts me up, and sets me on the counter. Without missing a beat he bends to suckle one breast while fondling the other. Bliss. I love this part of foreplay.

I close my eyes and recall Jessie, my last boyfriend. He was nice and an adequate lover. I ignore the fact that he cheated on me with my best friend. Well, my former best friend. I'll just pretend it's Jessie's cute blond head laving my nipple and not Attila the Zinn.

He switches seamlessly from one breast to the other. For a beginner, he's good. He must have been watching a lot of videos. His teeth scrape the tip a little too hard and there's a moment of pain that morphs into pleasure. I'm glad I'm sitting. That little move could make a girl weak in the knees.

"Let's try the little toys you picked." He reaches for the pair of red screws that look like they came straight out of the Inquisition. Tell me again why I grabbed these.

"Victoria. The rules," he prompts.

"Yes, Sir."

"My understanding is you simply screw one to each beautiful, pink nipple."

He acts as if he's done this a hundred times. I wonder how he practiced back on Zinn.

"I'll stop when it's tight." He screws a few turns and stops as soon as it's snug enough to stay on. Then repeats the task on the other side. He bobbles each to make certain they won't fall off. The gentle tug catches my attention.

Hey, this isn't so bad.

"Now I'm to tighten them an additional one-half turn each."

"Ouch."

"The manuals state some females like this."

"Well, I don't," I pout.

"There's supposed to be intense pleasure when I release the clamps."

"Is that like the old joke, 'doctor it hurts when I hit myself with a hammer'? The answer is to stop hitting yourself."

"You're not liking this?"

"The word hate would be more accurate," I simper.

He leans in to kiss me. His lips quest softly, his tongue plying mine, invading my mouth. He tastes sweet as he delves and explores, stroking responses from me. A hungry pulse of need jolts between my thighs. I'm breathless.

I order my hands to stay fisted at my sides. If they had a mind of their own they would be combing through his lustrous white hair. My tongue, however, is not responding to orders. It is dancing with his, enjoying the warmth of his mouth, quantifying his taste—minty sweet.

Minutes later, he pulls away. "How's our experiment?"

For a moment, I can't focus, then I realize he's asking about my nipples. He distracted me so well with his damn kisses I forgot about them.

He undoes each clamp and pulls them off. There's a burst of pain and then a heightened awareness. It feels kinda sexy, but my lips are sealed; I'll never tell him.

Just the ambient breeze makes me aware of the hard peaks standing at attention for everyone in the room to see. Kinda hard to hide, just like his big, pulsing purple cock.

"That's what all these implements are for; we'll discover what you like and what you don't."

"Let's put that one in the 'don't' pile."

"Duly noted."

He dips his head to lave my nipple. It zings right to my core. I see the attraction of these little torture devices. They heightened my sensitivity fivefold. I'll go to my grave carrying that secret. Oh my God, I hope I don't have to.

"You've done well, Victoria. You earned an hour alone in the bedroom." He strokes my head and walks to his chair.

"Yes, Sir." I wonder if he can hear my relief.

I scurry in and plop on the bed. There's absolutely nothing to do other than watch porn. I try every position, but can't get comfortable. I try to nap, but can't. I hate to admit it, but I'm wondering what he'll do next—more in anticipation than dread. This realization highlights just how fucked up I am.

"Victoria," his voice is so commanding I wonder if I should salute.

"Yes, Sir."

"Your hour is up and we have serious work to do. Come out here."

"Yes, Sir."

I shamble to the galley wondering if we have to go outside and scrape barnacles off the bow, or the hull, or whatever. What type of serious work is he talking about? I refuse to ask.

"I want to teach you how to orgasm on command." His silver eyes are serious and guileless, as if he wants to teach me how to bake bread, as if this is not the most insane sentence ever uttered.

What. The. Fuck?

"I shouldn't need to give you any more reminders about the rules. I probably should punish you right here and now, but perhaps you're fuzzy-headed from your nap. You are to respond 'yes, Sir' when I tell you something."

"Yes, Sir." He's still looking at me. "Yes, Sir. Twice, Sir. Are we even now?"

"You're riding the line between funny and sassy. Sassy will no longer be tolerated."

"Yes, Sir." I stifle the urge to curtsy. That might push him over the edge. One thing I know for certain, I don't want this male to punish me. The pleasure is enough to kill me.

"Orgasm on command may take the entire fourteen days for you to master."

I don't interrupt to remind him that we're down to the thirteen-day mark. I'll just keep that fun factoid to myself.

"I need to learn your response cycle. Then give you a command to orgasm when you're moments from orgasming. Your body will learn to respond to my command over its own desires."

He looks at me expectantly. "Do you have feedback?"

"No, Sir."

"Certainly you have thoughts, or have you done this before?"

"No, I haven't done this before," I snap. "My thoughts? One, it sounds clinical. And two, the word 'orgasm' isn't gonna do it for me. If you're expecting success, let's not doom it to failure. I don't want to be punished for not coming. Can we call it coming from now on?"

"I assumed that word was… lewd and not worthy of you."

"Well, whatever. It's the right word for this. My body doesn't work on command. Some days it's all I can do to wake up and get to class on time. Asking it to orgasm upon verbal command? *Your* verbal command? Your aspirations are too high, and I don't want to be penalized for something I'm not capable of."

"I will never punish you for not learning things quickly. Tonight I want to watch your sexual response cycle."

"I thought you did that when I was comatose."

"Yes." He frowns, pondering for a long time. "Let me apologize for that, Victoria. I was wrong. Let me repeat that because I want our relationship built on trust and I started on the wrong foot. There's no excuse. I read a lot and took the wrong advice. I've changed my methods and apologize for breaking trust before we even met. I regret that and I'm sorry."

I try to avoid eye contact with him as much as possible; I think it encourages him. But I risk a glance and see he's looking right at me—no-holds-barred staring. And he's contrite, serious. In my experience apologizing is hard for anybody, but apologizing for big, dominant Voxx must have cost him big-time.

"Yes, Sir." I hold the eye contact. I'm not certain I fully accept his apology, but I have to appreciate the spirit in which it was given.

"I don't want to scare you, Victoria. I don't wish to hurt you, nor do I wish to punish you. What I desire is the true bond that can exist between a Zinn and his human mate. I watched it all my life with my parents."

"Yes, Sir." Wow, he's doubling down on the kindness ploy. I hate to admit—it's working. His face is even more handsome when he's not ordering me around. The harsh set of his jaw relaxes and the parentheses that bracket his mouth draw my attention to his perfectly shaped lips.

"Go over there." He motions to the wall. I comply.

"Over our time together you will learn certain postures. I will teach you this one first. It's called Wall."

Catchy.

"Feet here." He points his toe two feet from the wall. "Arms above your head, hands on the wall." He stands behind me and presses my feet farther apart.

A hot spark of humiliation flashes through me. I'm on display, ass thrust out, center of gravity slightly off-kilter. Although the power dynamic has always been skewed between us—I woke up tied to a sex table for God's sake—I now feel even smaller in his presence.

"You will maintain this position until I say, 'free to move'. Do you understand?"

"Yes, Sir."

His warm hands slide up from my ankles along the outside of my legs to waist to underarms. After placing his hands on my shoulders, he glides downward back to my ankles. Now just the backs of his hands drift up the insides of my legs until they touch my outer lips. They lodge there for a moment.

The heat of his body penetrates my skin. The moment is caught in time. My total focus is on him. Silently, I urge him to touch my channel. But he moves up, caressing my ass with long, slow strokes. My inner walls quiver.

His huge hands span my waist. I'm not a little woman. There's something about those large hands covering me, claiming me, that make me feel owned. I hate to admit I like it, but the wetness trickling between my legs reveals the truth.

"You like my touch, Victoria." It's not a question.

He slides my hair to one side of my neck. How can that one movement be so sensual it awakens every nerve ending in its pathway?

Running his hands from my shoulders to wrists and up again, he takes his own sweet time, making certain to touch every inch of my skin. I hate my body right now because it's giving its allegiance from me to him. I can't control my own responses.

My breath catches, I feel my heartbeat thrum faster. It's confusing as hell that I can dislike everything about this situation—everything about him—and yet desire him at the same time.

His hands surround my throat, like a tall collar--another nonverbal testament to his ownership. Even as my mind rebels at the thought, my body oozes slickness, readying myself for his invasion.

He nudges my head forward, then moves the playing field to the front of my body. I guess he wants me to watch as his hands commence their slow, sensuous slide from ankles to inner thighs, then lodge in the crease between my thigh and my folds.

My mind plays a repeated mantra, psychically urging him to touch my core, I'm burning for it. Perhaps he heard me because he cups my sex. I hiss and dip my knees, desperately struggling for more pressure. He rips his hand away and scolds, "I told you not to move. Now I have to punish you."

I hate pain; I hate even the sound of the word punishment. Until today, that is. Until right this fucking moment. Because my inner submissive just woke up, ears pricked, wondering what the big Zinn plans to do to punish me. Her eager interest tells me she'll enjoy it.

"Yes, Sir." Instead of sounding indifferent or insolent, my tone is breathy and needy. I can't hide a thing from him.

"I've decided what I'm going to do. You'll have to wait and wonder for a few minutes."

Then his hands return to their slow stroking, awakening, claiming every inch of my body. My clit quivers for him, desperate for his touch. My internal walls clench and release, pretending there's something in my channel to clutch onto.

"Move your feet farther from the wall."

"Yes, Sir." I comply. Now my balance is off. My weight is on my hands; if they were pulled away I'd fall forward and break my nose. I'm at his mercy a million miles from home and the only thought drumming through my head is that I want him to penetrate me.

He strokes up over my belly to my rib cage and then circles my breasts where the orbs meet the chest. Even though it's not even an erogenous zone, I moan at his touch.

"That's right, Victoria. You can enjoy this," his warm breath brushes past my ear, giving me goosebumps. The flat of his tongue licks vertically up my neck to my hairline. I'm mesmerized. Waiting for his next move.

Those long, strong fingers that have been circling the edges of my breasts move closer to my nipples. *That's right, Voxx, it's like a target. Touch the bullseye.* But his movements are so slow. I groan again and bite my bottom lip. *Don't let me beg. Dear God, don't let me beg.*

Circling, circling, his touch sets fire to every nerve under my skin as he makes his way toward my aching, pebbled tips.

"Watch," he orders.

"Yes, Sir," I sound breathless.

Circling the aureole, both hands in unison, I observe as he pulls first one hand and then the other away. His hands return, palms glistening, I guess, from his saliva. He circles the flat of his palms on the tips of my nipples and I groan in surrender. Dear God, that feels so good.

His sensual attentions go on for long minutes as I fall deeper into a cocoon of lust. The bastard is such a quick study. What he's doing to my nipples is pure ecstasy. My inner thighs are slick with the testament to my need.

"Ready for your punishment?" he croons.

"Yes, Sir." My inner slut is eager to find out what he'll do.

"Beg, Victoria. Beg me to give you release."

Shit. I hate him. He's gone back to plucking, twisting, and scraping. I'm weak with wanting him.

"I'll wait," he husks into my ear.

I can, too. I'll outwait him. I'm strong.

His right hand rolls my nipple once more, then slides down my body so slowly I think the delay will kill me. His warm hand cups my sex—kind of. It's hovering a millimeter above my flesh. I can feel the warmth, but no touch—none.

"I forbid you to move," his voice is like iron.

His hand is so close to me I feel the heat. I'm desperate. There's a vicious war going on inside my head. My inner slut wants to beg, my inner drill sergeant forbids it.

Voxx taps the tip of my clit just firm enough for me to feel it, yet that one motion sets off an earthquake throughout my body and emotions. I cry out, the swift touch was ecstasy. My core is quivering. I can't take much more of this. I've never been a quitter, but I want to give in to him.

His left hand is still working my nipple, keeping me riding the edge. His right hand still hovers near my sex, reminding me that any second I could have relief if I were to but say the word.

"Please." The word is out of my mouth before I give myself permission to say it, but relief floods me. Now I will get my release.

"Please? Victoria, your punishment was clear. I told you to beg."

No. I'm not going to beg. That's more than I can bear. As I argue with myself, his right hand leaves its post and returns to my breast. I immediately miss the warmth and promise of the hand that had been so close to my sex.

How did I lose myself in less than two days? How could I let this happen?

His fingers are more insistent now, plucking harder, twisting more vigorously. Instead of repelling me, it sets off a cataclysm of need down below.

I can't do it. I can't let this go on any longer.

"I'm begging."

"More words, Victoria. Say who you're begging from, and what you want."

I don't debate with myself for one more second. The decision's already made. Okay, I can debase myself even more.

"Sir, I beg you, make me come."

"More," it's a seductive whisper, his mouth so close to my ear his breath warms me there.

"Sir, please, Voxx from Zinn, penetrate me, make me come."

"More."

"Sir, I'm begging, do whatever you want as long as you make me come."

"As you wish." He lifts me into his arms, strides to our bed, and sets me in the middle. "Legs apart," he orders as he prowls between them from the foot of the bed.

He grabs my hand and places it on my clit, then positions himself inches from the action. Somewhere in the hazy recesses of my brain, I remember he wanted to see my sexual response. I guess the time is now.

"Make yourself feel good. Don't come until I tell you," his voice is firm.

He doesn't have to ask me twice. I reach down and circle my happy spot, already close to coming. My heels reach higher until they touch my ass, which lifts off the mattress in anticipation of release.

I've already completely debased myself, so I think nothing of saying, "Sir, when I come would you put your fingers in me?"

Two fingers immediately begin circling my slick entrance. Fuck, that's so good. "More." Then I remember, "Please, Sir."

If I wasn't on orgasm restriction, I would come right now. But I hold off. "May I come, Sir?"

"Wait."

My bottom teeth are biting my lip so hard I wonder if I've drawn blood. My stomach and thigh muscles are quivering.

"Please, please," my voice is plaintive, desperate. "Please, may I come, Sir?"

"Come," he commands. And I do. The orgasm hits like a bucking bronc, tearing loud moans from me even as my muscles spasm in waves of blissful release. He plunges two fingers into me with the perfect rhythm to both fulfill me and extend the bliss. It's the longest, most powerful orgasm I've ever had, and aftershocks continue for another full minute or more.

I float back down, fully in my body, taking long moments to breathe. Then I open my eyes and see my purple nemesis looking at me as if I'm a bug pinned to a mat for his inspection. I fucking hate him. Even worse—I fucking hate myself. I'm weak. I was easily manipulated. My own body betrayed me. I could kill him right now if I had the means.

He lies down next to me and hugs my back to his front. Thank goodness for small favors. At least I don't have to look him in the eye, those beautiful silver eyes. His arm is slung across my waist; I'm stiff in his arms. I'm filled with loathing of both him and myself.

He pets my head and strokes my hair. "Such a good girl. You must be tired. I'll wash you and you can go to sleep."

He brings a bowl of warm water and a washcloth and smoothes my sweat-dampened hair and face. He cleans my skin and wipes the fluid from between my legs. I clamp my eyes closed. If I look at him for one more second, I won't be able to control my urge to hit him, which will only result in more punishment. I can't handle that right now.

After setting the bowl under the bed, he turns off the lights and spoons me. I know what's happening inside that purple cranium of his. He thinks we're dating, and he just gave his special lady the time of her life. He has no idea the only thought pulsing through my brain is murder. Maybe he should know. Maybe he'll let me go home early if he knows just how much I despise him.

"What about my ten minutes?" I ask, my tone tight. I'm foreshadowing what's coming next, getting him ready for the frosty blast of my hatred.

"My ten minutes of honesty? Sir?"

"Right, of course, Victoria. You may speak freely for ten minutes starting now."

"I can say whatever I want without punishment? I can call you Voxx, not Sir? Just checking out the rules, Sir, before we begin."

"Yes, those were the ground rules I agreed upon." He turns up the lights and I turn on my side to face him.

I'm getting ready to excoriate him, tell him how much I hate him, drop the "F" bomb a hundred or so times when that angel they joke about appears. The one that's supposed to be on your shoulder? Yeah, her.

I've never had that feeling before, but a thought from the far recesses of my brain catches my attention enough for me to clamp my lips shut.

Where will it get you to ream him a new one? My angel asks. *Being bitchy isn't going to get you released early. Creating a more adversarial atmosphere will only cause heartache— yours. In the form of punishment.*

The way to get out of here early is to outsmart him. He's a jerk, but when he doesn't feel compelled to punish you, he's been reasonable. Get to know him. The better you know him, the higher the likelihood you'll have the ammunition you need to convince him to let you go. You went into the legal profession for a reason, you can be persuasive when you want.

My angel's right. I need to use these ten minutes far more wisely than telling him how much I hate him. I need to gather information.

"Why me, Voxx. Why did you pick me?" I hold his gaze in mine.

"I thought you wanted to have ten minutes to speak your true feelings."

"The deal was for ten minutes of just Tori and Voxx. I want to get to know you." The glance I give him is genuine. This might be my only ticket off this ship.

His brows furrow, he's skeptical, but then he shrugs and sits up, his back against the headboard. I sit up and face him, my legs crossed with a pillow over my lap. I want this to be a serious discussion.

"I searched the Internet for years before I turned thirty and became eligible for the lottery. I honed my methods, knowing that any eligible females would probably find a mate before I could choose them. But through trial and error, I learned what I was looking for.

"When I became eligible and I stumbled upon your profile, it was obvious you were the one. I quit looking after I found you. You were at University, but hadn't started your legal studies yet. Every day I jumped on your social media to make certain you hadn't bound yourself to a male. It's forbidden by the Compact to take another male's mate."

All hale the patriarchy. You can snatch me, but not if I'm bound to a man. Ugh.

"But what was it about me that made you decide I was the one?"

For the first time since I've known him, the corners of his lips tip into an easy smile. His eyebrows quirk as if to ask 'isn't it obvious'? "You're everything any male could want, Tori." His big hand swallows mine as he grabs it and rubs his thumb along my knuckles.

"You were smart, kind, motivated, always bolstering your friends when they were having a bad day. You worked hard to put yourself through school."

He smoothes a stray lock of hair behind my ear. I tell myself he's not expressing genuine affection, but it sure feels tender, especially with that warm gaze searching my face, waiting for me to reciprocate.

"I appreciated that your media wasn't crammed with pictures of yourself, but the ones you posted were always modest and happy—and beautiful. You were the prettiest female on Earth. I woke up every morning and saw what you were thinking about, what you were busy with before I went to work. You became part of the fabric of my life."

A part deep inside myself is skeeved out by the depth and breadth of his stalking. Another part is flattered to think a secret admirer knows everything about me and still likes me. And he thinks I'm beautiful.

My hand is still grasped in his. It's warm and gentle and wants nothing from me. It's the first time I've felt relaxed in his presence.

"Tell me why having a mate is so important to you, Voxx." My first question was just to warm him up, get his defenses down. This is the question that will help me talk my way off this vessel.

"We only have thirty-two seconds left, Tori. We'll have to leave that for tomorrow.
Anything else you want to say before your time is up?"

I'll never like you, Voxx from Zinn, I tell him in the privacy of my mind. *"I'll tolerate you and follow your rules until Day Fourteen when you take me back to Earth.*

What I say is, "Thanks for sharing, Sir."

Our eyes meet for a moment before he turns out the lights. Something unexpected shimmers between us. A gossamer thread of connection. Those ethereal silver eyes speak to me as he tenderly eases me down and pulls the covers up to my chin. His considerate actions make me hunger to know the answer to my last question.

I can't deny the feeling of calm settling over me as his arm reaches around me and pulls me close to spoon me. The feeling of comfort I have just being next to him? I'll have to squelch that. I need to stay distant, to nurture my hatred. I'll start first thing in the morning. Right now, I snuggle closer to him and let the deep rhythm of his breathing relax me.

Voxx

I've imagined this night since puberty when I gained a true understanding of the lottery process and what would happen if I was lucky enough to be aboard an Earthbound vessel for the fourteen glorious days of the Quest.

I read many books, talked to my aunts, questioned my parents endlessly, but nothing prepared me for this. Fifteen minutes ago, it was bliss being able to fulfill my mate. Frankly, it was easier than I'd thought. Pleasuring Victoria came naturally to me. And she's so sensual, so compliant— exactly as I knew she would be.

Just now, Victoria showed an interest in me. I think her anger toward me is dwindling. Our bond will only grow stronger over the coming weeks and beyond.

I warned myself before I took her. I knew the reality would be different than the expectation. Watching her from afar couldn't be the same as being in the confines of the *Drayant* with an angry captive. The last two days have been a pleasant surprise.

She hasn't warmed to me—I didn't expect that so soon. Neither did I expect to enjoy her so much despite her resistance. She thinks I have no sense of humor, but I see her quick wit peeking out from time to time.

Her sensuality? It exceeds my wildest expectations, and we've only begun to explore her boundaries. I'm going to be attentive and diligent, even as I maintain a firm hand. I'm going to make this work.

Day Three

Victoria

I felt like a traitor last night. After I extracted information from him like a super spy, he pulled me tight and kissed my head until I fell asleep.

Oh well, all's fair in love and war, and this is war. I have enough to worry about. Like getting through today with my self-esteem intact.

"Review the rules," he orders as he cooks breakfast. The soft Tori/Voxx moment of last night is history.

It scares me that after only these few days it feels normal to be prancing around naked on a spaceship. He's wearing a towel around his waist, I guess he doesn't want anything splattering on his man-bits. Although 'bits' doesn't describe it accurately. How about man-log?

"Victoria!" he barks.

"Yes, Sir. Sorry, Sir. I was just making certain I would get it right." I'm getting to be an excellent liar.

"Don't lie."

Well, maybe not such an excellent liar.

I recite the rules, and he tells me I'm a good girl. Maybe during tonight's ten minutes I'll let him in on the little secret that I don't enjoy being treated like a female dog. Then again, maybe I like his praise. Jeez, I'm so fucked up.

He feeds me little morsels, which are delicious, in between his bites.

I glance out the huge front window into space. I haven't quite gotten used to any of it: the vastness, or the silent beauty, or the fact that there's no difference between day and night. I wonder where Earth is. Being out here reminds me of how tiny I am, how alone I am in the universe.

He feeds me the last bite of breakfast, then lifts me off my perch on the bar and sets me in front of the sink. I make short work of cleanup after he instructs me on how to use the 'cleanbox'.

"Wall," he instructs. I guess playtime is over. Or maybe it's starting, I can't keep anything straight anymore.

When I assume the correct position, he says, "Good girl," then "I want to find your G-spot."

A little bark of a laugh escapes my mouth. I mean, really, we just finished breakfast. He doesn't crack a smile.

"Yes, Sir."

"We'll start with a new position, Present."

"Yes, Sir." I don't like it already.

"Get on your back on the bed, arms above your head, legs pointing at the two corners, knees straight."

Fuck.

"Yes, Sir." I scramble to comply; he doesn't sound like he's in a lenient mood.

"Palms up," he corrects. "Arch your back, I want to enjoy your breasts. Good girl."

Someday I'll have to figure out why my core liquifies when he calls me a good girl.

He stalks over to the wall of torture. I snuck a look yesterday and other than the vibrators, I wish all the implements of destruction would be sucked out the garbage jettison into deep space. Please, please, please, Voxx, pick up the bullet vibe.

He grabs a whippy thing.

I went through the obligatory 'I want a horse' phase in grade school. I'm pretty sure the contraption in his hand is a riding crop. He's swishing it through the air—it makes a whistling sound.

That lubrication I was worrying about? Gone. Evaporated. I'm sure I'm dry as a bone down there. I'm using every ounce of willpower I possess to keep my legs open to maintain my position.

"You look terrified, Victoria. I'm not going to hit you today."

Did he say 'today'? He couldn't have just stopped at 'I'm not going to hit you'?

After disengaging something, he pulls the bed away from the wall so he now has 360-degree access. He steps behind me and I can't see him. My eyes flare wide and I'm panting.

"Please don't hit me, Sir. Please."

"I've never lied to you, Victoria. I've already said I won't hit you. The intended outcome of this exercise is for you to come. Try to relax."

"Yes, Sir."

He strokes my head for long minutes. Maybe I do like all the doggy references because petting my head feels heavenly.

"You're relaxing. That's good." The crop caresses my ankle. The supple leather takes a leisurely stroll up the outside of my thigh, up my body, across my throat, and down the other side.

"Deeper breaths will help."

When the crop reaches my other ankle, it retraces its journey up, over, and down. Okay, I can do this. Piece of cake.

He completes another full circuit and I'm in a cocoon of calm. He's continued to pet my head the entire time.

Now the crop crosses from outer ankle to inner, and the crop makes its way up as far as it will go, travels across my cleft, and down to the other ankle. That one little stroke across my private spaces, barely a brush, set my body trembling.

He completes the pass again. This time I arch toward the leather.

"Like the crop, Victoria?"

"Yes, Sir."

"I'd hoped you would. Relax into it. No pain. Although maybe some interesting surprises."

After several more circuits of this, each more intimate than the last, he flips the crop in his hand so he's holding the shaft right above the floppy leather square on the end. The black leather handle now points toward me.

It learns the circuit: ankle to cleft to ankle. On its third trip, it stops, upright, at the current center of my universe. Its vertical shaft presses against my clit. A hiss escapes my throat.

The crop continues its journey down to my ankle, back up, then lodges hard against my slit again. After another trip, Voxx provocatively slides it up and down against me. I use all my willpower not to bend my knees and press against the leather shaft. I can't, however, suppress my moan of desire.

Voxx removes the crop, then dangles the glistening leather shaft over my face. "Suck this into your mouth."

It's maybe 10:30 in the morning and a purple alien wants me to suck an inanimate object dripping with my own juices. I'm completely repulsed and can't wait for him to press it between my lips.

"Yes, Sir." I don't even pretend reluctance.

"Very good girl," he praises as I obediently open my mouth. It's my very first 'very' and for some sick-as-shit reason, I'm inordinately proud.

"Suck it," he instructs.

I do. Like a good girl, a very good girl.

He pulls the crop out and uses the wet handle to tantalize my erect nipples. The foreign feel of the wet leather, the tang of the smell in the air, and the kinkiness of the moment have me arching my back in desire. Having to keep my legs apart, not being able to bend them, the empty desperation between my legs—these things have set me ablaze.

Voxx bends, his lips inches from mine. His eyes are beautiful. They're piercing and otherworldly and appear to look into my soul. They look as desperate for me as I am for him.

"Tell me you want my kiss."

My eyes open wider. Do I?

"Only say you want it if it's true. Do you?"

His lips are perfect, thick and pouty and magenta. At this moment I do want him to kiss me. God help me, I do.

"Yes, Sir."

His hip settles on the bed next to mine. He's abandoned the crop, because both his hands lodge in my hair, clutching my head, pulling me close. His tongue invades me—it's not tender or tentative. It's bold and demanding. My tongue dances with his.

His taste? Divine. I want more. More of everything.

I tip my head back and ask, breathless, "Can I leave the position?"

"Yes."

I grab his head and pull him closer. I stroke his tongue, then bite his lips and lift my heels to my ass, splaying myself open for him.

I want to beg him to fuck me, but I can't. Not because I don't want it. Not because I'm embarrassed. Not because it would be a blatant admission that part of me likes—no loves—being his little fuck-toy. But because if I do, it might jerk him out of this dream and snap him back to his mean, demanding self.

He slides down my body, shoulders his way between my legs, and licks me from core to clit with the flat of his tongue.

"Sir," I hiss in pleasure. A frisson of fear slices through me, I'm not even sure if I'm allowed to talk. But he doesn't correct me, so I focus on the delightful, amazing things he's doing to me.

Flicking! He's flicking my clit with his tongue. Turning me on from horny to blasting out of the stratosphere. And it's perfect, not too hard, not too soft, not right on it, but on the side, just where I like it.

He pulls back for a moment, blowing on me, allowing me to grab a breath. Every single brain cell is focused on what he's doing to me down there.

When he hunkers down and licks me again, I'm more sensitized than before.

A finger slips into me. "Oh, God!" One finger and I'm almost there. I'm quivering, I could explode in a second.

I remind myself I'm not supposed to come until he tells me. In the past, with every man I've been with, I've struggled to orgasm. Supreme irony that right now I'm struggling to contain myself.

I begin rocking against him and moaning. Even though this is his first taste of my lady bits, he owns it like a boss. He nips my upper thigh, scraping my tender flesh with his teeth.

"You taste so good," he croons, then pulls out his finger long enough to press his tongue deep inside me. "So good," he repeats as he slips in two fingers and then sucks my clit into the warmth of his mouth.

I shift from heaven to bliss. "Sir. Too good. Perfect. So good." I sing his praises when I should be hating this and demanding he stop. But he won't. I know it. His only goal is my pleasure, he's made that clear.

His soft slurping noises, knowing he thinks I taste divine, that he's enjoying this more than the finest dessert, shred my last inhibitions. My moan comes out as a frenzied growl, which whips him up, his fingers quickening their rhythm.

Those long fingers are on a mission. They explore and find the spot deep inside me that sends me into orbit. "Sir!" The ecstasy is so intense it's shocking. "Please, let me come." I can't last even one second more.

"Wait." What is it about his deep, commanding voice, denying my strangled request that makes me even hornier?

His hand slows for a moment even though his mouth doesn't miss a beat. I sink into the bed, panting. My fingers clutch the sheets as I try to focus on anything other than my achy, desperate need for release.

He growls, a deep, rumbling, masculine sound that vibrates from my clit to my very soul.

"Sir." I'm panting, tossing my head back and forth, focusing on self-control. Numbers. I try multiplication tables, the twelves are hard. I get stuck at twelve times seven and realize my arousal has backed down a notch. Okay, note to self, this works.

His fingers get busy again, working the magic spot inside me even as his mouth and tongue are delivering merciless pleasure.

"Please, Sir. Begging."

"Come for me," he commands against my clit.

And I do. Cataclysm. Explosion. Convulsion. The pulses roll through my body in waves. My molars clamp down along with every muscle in my body as I experience a level of release I never imagined possible.

Tears are rolling down my cheeks, it was just too intense to tolerate. It was staggering. The feelings are too overwhelming. Almost unbearable except they were wonderful.

Voxx is still down there, his mouth on my clit, his fingers unmoving inside me. I reach down to urge him up, but he starts again.

"No. Too much," I gasp as he flicks my clit gently with just the tip of his tongue. "Too much," I say with less conviction as the feeling morphs from too much to just right.

How did he figure out how to own my body? It's as if he has an instruction manual. He ratcheted way back and is coaxing my little clit back to life with tiny licks and slurps and sucks. I realize I'm fully back in the game when my hips begin their familiar rhythm. He realizes, too, because his hand pulses into me again.

It takes only moments before I come again. Not the cataclysmic explosion of a moment ago, but a deep release that starts in my belly and rolls down to my toes as every muscle in my body tightens and relaxes over and over.

When it's finally finished, I've come five or six times. They blended together and it was hard to tell if it was three little ones or one long extended one. And who cares, anyway? Why was I counting? It was bliss.

He slides up next to me and cups his hand possessively on my sex.

"I guess you found it," I say.

"What?"

"I believe you were looking for my G-spot."

"Perhaps," he says. He's got a relaxed smile on his face as he leans down to kiss me.

Come to think of it, how can he be relaxed when we've been swimming in a pool of sexual excitement for days? I've come dozens of times, and he's gotten no release. I read the Interstellar Compact, it didn't prohibit penetration.

God knows, his cock works. I glance down at it. It's deep purple, pulsing with every heartbeat. Weeping a lavender pearl of desire.

"I shouldn't care..." *Because I still despise you*, I think. "But don't Zinns need to come?" It's a ridiculous question, really, because the poor thing looks ready to explode.

"There are reasons…," he drifts off, then continues, "According to the manuals, you're not ready."

He kisses my forehead and saunters to the bathroom. Oooh, he's jacking off in there.

Did he say I'm not ready? Maybe he just doesn't want to get me pregnant. Far be it from me to tell him I'm on birth control and he could safely fuck me all day long. I don't need to encourage him.

This moment of quiet leaves me far too much time to reflect on what just happened in this bed and what's been happening since my abduction. I kissed this man, er, male. I kissed those perfect lips and begged him to make me come.

If he stalked out of the bathroom right now and tried to fuck me I'd be hard-pressed to reject him. I practically purr when he pets my head. I've been dripping wet for him since we met. The motherfucker kidnapped me from my bed and took liberties with my body and bosses me around. He's thought all this out and has names for the sex positions he puts me into for fuck's sake.

If I was a normal person, I'd ransack the vessel right this moment, looking for a ray gun to kill him with. But my deepest desire is for him to come back and put his mouth on me again. No. Correct that. All I want right now is for him to shove his cock in me.

I'm sick and weak and don't deserve any better than this because no self-respecting woman should want anything other than to kill him for what he's done. What would my mom say, or my friends? Gloria Steinem, Betty Friedan, Susan B. Anthony, all those feminists who risked their safety and comfort so that women like me could have better lives would shake their heads at spineless little Victoria.

Closing my eyes, I take a deep breath and promise to be more resolute in my hate. I will resist him. I will call him Sir and do what he orders to save my skin. But when he asks if I want a kiss or to be fucked I swear by all that's holy, I will refuse. He said I'm not ready for his cock? Damn right.

He exits the little adjoining bathroom, toweling his hair. "Want a shower?"

"Yes," I snip as I press past him and shut the door. I can't hide here too long, the shower turns off after ten minutes, and there's only so long I can pretend to use the can.

When I re-emerge, he's not in bed. He's in his captain's chair on the bridge looking busy and captainy and handsome. Nope, not going there.

He's quiet and his jaw is tight. "Come here."

"Yes, Sir."

Looks like harsh, domineering Sir has returned with a vengeance.

"With alacrity," he barks.

"Yes, Sir." I hurry.

"Get a blanket from the bedroom closet and bring it here."

"Yes, Sir."

I scramble to comply. He seems pissed and I don't want to get on his last nerve. I return, blanket in hand, within a minute.

"Fold it four times and place it here." He points to the floor at his side.

After I do as I'm told, I stand, waiting for his next order.

"Your next position is Kneel. It is only because I am a kind master that I give you something to kneel on. Should you anger me or misbehave, I will remove the blanket."

"Yes, Sir."

"Kneel, tops of your feet on the floor. Sit on your legs, cross your hands behind your waist. Normally your eyes should be cast down, but I don't require that at this time."

"Yes, Sir." I follow his instructions to the letter, but he finds fault with my feet and hand positions and chastises me for not keeping my back straight enough.

"I'll release you in ten minutes. It's hard to maintain any of your postures. You'll get better with time and practice."

I bite my tongue and contain the urge to point out that I only have eleven more days of this shit.

He strokes my hair. I remind myself he's the enemy and I should not take one ounce of pleasure from his abhorrent touch. I pretend not to notice that my core is leaking in response to his gentle caress. I forbid myself to lean into his hand; I keep my back straight and eyes ahead.

The view out those windows is dazzling. I allow myself a moment of sadness; it's a shame they'll wipe all of this from my mind when they transport me home. I'd love to recall the beauty of a blue nebula from the vantage point of space.

I won't miss this, though. The aching in my knees, the humiliation of my constant nudity, the fear when he barks an order at me. *Oh*, the scathing voice inside my head rebukes, *but you'll miss the heat in his eyes when you catch him staring at you like you're the most alluring thing he's ever seen. You'll miss the way your core weeps at his softest touch. You'll miss the pounding orgasms he just gave you in bed, making you come until you couldn't take any more. You'll miss those.*

"You're free to move," his voice has lost its bite; his hand's still sifting through my hair.

I move the blanket forward a few inches to avoid the hard arm of the chair and lay my head above his knee.

"What a good girl," he praises.

Why did I do this? I'm certain I have some space sickness that's caused insanity. I hope it isn't permanent.

In a moment, I'll find something to do, although I want to avoid the porn-laden vids and books. But just for a moment I'll close my eyes and soak up the… I don't know what I'm soaking up from those long, strong fingers of his.

"I thought you might want to speak to my mother today." His words were soft and without malice. Their effect, however, was like an incendiary bomb. Why would I want to speak to his mother? She's a traitor. She left Earth willingly. To be a sex slave. What could she possibly say that I'd want to hear?

"She's been exactly where you've been, Victoria. You might find a chat helpful."

"She's been exactly where I've been, like Iowa? Because she couldn't have been here. She couldn't have been sitting at some purple asshole's feet being forced into positions and marched around nude and manipulated like a fuckdoll."

Oh holy shit. All of that flew out of my mouth and I'm going to get punished. I can't stop the torrent, though. "Certainly she's never been stolen from her bed and had a vibrator placed on her most private spaces without permission and screamed in ecstasy and hated every minute of it.

"Sir, I'm sorry. Please don't beat me with a whip. I couldn't help myself."

Oh my God, how can I talk to him like that and live to tell the tale? A giant fist squeezes my chest. I think I'm going to pass out from fear.

Voxx

She's leaning as far from me as possible without falling over backward. Her eyes are round in terror. My little Victoria, the female I pleasured with my mouth until she screamed in ecstasy less than an hour ago is looking at me like I'm the enemy. For every step forward, I take at least one step back.

Somehow I don't think it would be helpful to tell her my mother has been exactly where she is. Exactly. This is the family space vessel. Thirty-four years ago I have no doubt she sat at my father's feet next to this very captain's chair.

"My mother understands what it's like to be abducted, Victoria. She's as close as you'll get to having a friend during this difficult period in your life. What have you got to lose?"

She starts to rise, but I order, "Kneel," and she complies. No more docile Victoria, warm and curled next to me at my feet. Now her back is straight, her jaw is tight, and her eyes are cast down, just as I detailed earlier. I hate it.

"I rescind my offer. I forbid you to speak to my mother. My mother is a warm, compassionate woman who would not take kindly to anyone who calls her son a purple asshole.

"Nor do I, Victoria. I have been extremely lenient allowing you the ten-minute period at night. Now you've broken a rule and must be punished."

"Yes, Sir." I can't tell if she's truly contrite or scared of my wrath.

I need to determine a proper punishment. It will also do her good to wait anxiously for my pronouncement. Her rising panic is palpable as she wonders what I'll do.

"Get into a new position. It's called Down. Move there." I motion straight ahead of me. "Your head toward the windows, lie on your front, flat on the floor, face down, hands behind your back."

"Yes, Sir," her voice is so soft I can barely hear her.

I never wanted to place her in this position. It's degrading. "Legs wide, Victoria." I slide one foot forward to press her legs open wider. "Head down, lips on the floor."

She's crying. She has to learn. That is why we're given fourteen days. The process needs time to allow her to get the hate out of her system and embrace her desire to submit to my dominance. All the books predicted a difficult initiation.

The position manipulates my thoughts. I can focus on nothing other than her ass and pink folds when I look at her this way.

"Reflect on what you did wrong. I'll allow you additional movement in ten minutes."

"Yes, Sir." She's lying so still I can barely see her breathe. Her position is exactly as I specified, although her compliance brings me no joy.

I relieve my raging hard-on in the restroom while she remains on the floor. The sexual release helps me clear my head so I can deal with her calmly. The female must trust the male to be in control.

Up until now, I've been in control for both of us. It's the one thing I've done correctly since she came on board. I won't break that streak now.

"You can scoot back and put your hands straight ahead of you on the floor if you're experiencing pain. You can change from one position to the other at will for the duration of your punishment."

"Yes, Sir." Her voice is wavery from crying.

I've behaved like a bad parent, always threatening punishment, then avoiding the severe decree. I will follow through this time; she must learn.

Bending, I place the thick, inflexible collar on her neck. She sucks in a gasp but maintains her position. I withhold my usual 'good girl'.

"Have you had experience with anal penetration?" My voice is firm. I don't want to fill her with false hope of leniency.

She shakes her head. I press my foot between her shoulder blades. My touch is light and couldn't cause pain. It's meant to remind her I'm in control.

"Use your words, Victoria. This position requires your mouth on the floor."

"No, Sir," her quiet voice is muffled.

"In a moment I'll ask you a question. You will have permission to speak freely as long as your statement contains no profanity and does not cast aspersions upon me or anyone I hold dear. Do you understand the parameters?"

"Yes, Sir."

"And the limits of my patience?"

"Yes, Sir."

"What are your feelings and attitudes about anal penetration?"

"I've never wanted to try it, Sir." On that, she sounds clear.

"Then this will be your punishment."

She sobs once and I apply a slight bit more pressure between her shoulders. She cuts herself off instantly. I bite back my urge to tell her she's a good girl.

Stalking to the wall of implements, I make certain she hears every footstep and notices the time I take choosing the proper tools. I set all the chosen toys on the bedside table, then return to her on the floor of the bridge.

Slipping a black hood over her head, I glimpse her terrified face, then pull her to stand and lead her to the bed.

"You will assume the same position on the bed. This is for my physical comfort, not yours."

"Yes, Sir." She scrambles to comply.

I take a moment to plan my strategy. My goal for this exercise is twofold. She has to learn I'm the dominant in this relationship. She must learn she can't curse at me or disrespect my mother. I hope by the end of this she won't even dare to *think* of me as a purple asshole.

On the other hand, I don't want her to hate my touch, nor do I want to taint anal sex for her. I want it to be a source of genuine pleasure for her—and us—for years to come.

"Open your legs wider."

"Yes, Sir."

Nudging her hip with mine, I settle onto the bed next to her. I rub her ass gently, then knead it until her breathing calms.

"Tell me who's in charge on this vessel?"

"You, Sir."

I pull the hood off her head and use it to wipe her tear-stained face.

"Tell me again."

"You're in charge, Sir."

"That's what the collar is to remind you of. I thought you could remember without it, but it needs to remain on."

"Yes, Sir."

"Thank me for helping you remember your place. It will help you avoid punishment in the future."

"Thank you, Sir."

"I'll give you a moment, take as long as you need. You tell me, Victoria, what should your punishment be if you call your Sir names in the future?"

She considers for a long time. "Whatever you see fit, Sir."

"That is an excellent response, Victoria, and at another time I might accept it as an answer. But not now. Tell me a proper punishment."

She considers for a moment. "The nipple clamps, Sir. One full turn tighter. And…" She pauses for a full minute. "I believe I saw another pair of them, Sir. One on my… clit." This last word came out more like a breath than a spoken word.

I'd never have imagined she'd come up with this punishment. It makes my cock bob in excitement. With her splayed out in front of me, it's clear this 'punishment' excites her, too. I see liquid-desire glistening near her entrance.

I'm still rubbing her ass cheeks, calming her. Reaching between her wide-spread legs, I cup her mound, my wrist and forearm pressing along her channel.

"Who does this belong to?"

"You, Sir."

"Say it."

"This belongs to you, Sir."

"You're studying to be a barrister, Victoria. Use those powers of persuasion to tell me in five different ways, with clarity and conviction who this belongs to." Still cupping her mons, I press my thumb into her pussy as far as it can reach. She sucks in a breath.

"My body belongs to you. My pussy belongs to you." She pauses for a moment.

"Every sentence should end with 'Sir', don't you think?"

"My body belongs to you, Sir. My pussy belongs to you, Sir. My... cunt belongs to you, Sir. You can do what you want with my body, Sir. You can put what you want in my body, Sir. You own my body, Sir."

I pull out my thumb and slide two fingers into her slick opening. Pulsing in and out of her, I say, "You exceeded expectations, Victoria. That was six. Touch yourself until you come. When you do, I want you to thank me."

Her right hand wiggles under her. As she works her clit, I slam my fingers into her. She doesn't shy from my touch, she reaches back to feel the impact.

"Tell me when you're close. You still need my permission."

"Yes, Sir." Her bottom reaches to receive every thrust of my fingers. I slide her wetness to her ass in several passes, then rest my thumb on her little pucker. She doesn't miss a beat as her hand grinds her clit and her bottom thrusts up on my fingers.

"Close, Sir."

"Wait."

"Yes, Sir."

My thrusts don't slow, I want her to struggle to maintain. Slipping a third finger in, I feel her stretch as she accommodates me.

"Close, close, close," she pants.

"Wait."

The room is filled with her scent and her grunts and the slapping of wet flesh. I slide my thumb into her back hole up to the first knuckle as I say "Come."

My lovely Victoria bucks against me, thrusting her pussy back onto my fingers, pressing her backside onto my thumb and screaming in release. She takes long moments to swim back to the surface of full consciousness.

"Thank you, Sir. Thank you."

"Kiss my palm."

She does. Instantly. Without question or hesitation.

"Lick these clean." I stick out my middle and index fingers. Obedient Victoria sucks them into her mouth and licks. "As if they're my cock, Victoria." She complies, bobbing her head up and down while looking me straight in the eyes.

I slide into bed and cuddle her, her head rests on my chest, my chin on her scalp.

"Have you been punished enough for calling me a purple asshole?"

She breaks away from my gentle embrace as her eyes flare to mine. I know this look. She's wondering if my question is a trick.

"I… I don't know?"

"You have, Victoria. You've been punished enough. Lie back down."

"Yes, Sir."

"I'm going to teach you how to cook my favorite dinner, then I'll let you pick a toy for us to play with before bed."

Victoria

I'm crazy. Completely insane. I have morphed from a competent, normal law student to a sex-crazed, desperate wanton slut in three days—less than three days. I've lost my mind and have nowhere to turn.

I need a friend and I have none in space. Voxx offered me one option and I need to take it. I hate his mother. I've never met her, but I hate her with a passion. First of all, she birthed the bastard. Second, she raised him to be the extreme motherfucker that he is. She caved in to her own purple asshole and flew off to some shitty planet on the other side of the universe to play S&M games for the rest of her life.

That's on her.

But I need someone to talk to before I completely lose my mind.

"Sir." I sidle up behind him in the galley as he pulls food from the pantry and cold box.

"Yes, Victoria."

"Sir, I would like to take you up on your offer."

He cocks an eyebrow.

"To speak with your mother."

He turns to give me his full attention, his brow lowered. "Are you scheming? Are you planning something nefarious to hurt my mother's feelings? I can't express in words what a bad choice that would be." His lips thin into a flat line and his eyes slit in anger.

"No, Sir. You were right when you said I needed a friend. I know she isn't really a friend. She has a dog in the fight, after all, I'm sure she wants me to choose you on Choosing Day. But I could use someone to talk to who isn't…" I want to say, 'abusing me on a daily basis', but I merely finish with, "You."

He inspects me for another minute, then nods his head. "I'll comm her and see if she has time in two hours. If so, you can speak with her after dinner."

"Thank you, Sir."

I've never been a great cook. Law school is demanding. The best I do when I'm not catching food on the run is making ramen noodles, house-brand mac and cheese, or PB&J sandwiches.

Voxx teaches me how to make a Zinn version of beef stroganoff. It's not gourmet, but I did a decent job with the cooking, dinner was edible, and Voxx seemed inordinately happy with me which is, after all, what my world revolves around these days.

Voxx hands me a colorful caftanish robe he pulled out of a drawer. I'd assumed it would be a visual call and wondered if he would make me stand naked while I spoke with his mom.

"You can make the call in our room. I will turn off the cameras and microphones. Rest assured, you will have complete privacy. I hope it's productive."

"Hello, Victoria. It's nice to meet you. I'm Jennifer," she says when she comes on screen. She smiles at me like she's thrilled to speak with me. She's pretty. I guess I shouldn't be surprised that we look a lot alike. They say men marry their mothers. Her hair is long and brown, her eyes are blue, and her face is heart-shaped, just like mine.

"Um, pleased to meet you?"

"I understand. This must be so awkward for you. I would have killed to have someone to talk to when I was in your shoes. My Master's mother was dead."

Oh my God. Did she call her husband Master? I don't want to judge her. We each get to make our own choices in life, but ugh. I'll die before I call Voxx Master.

"Thank you for speaking with me."

"Did you have questions?"

"Um, I don't know what to ask."

"Can I just ramble then?"

Her cornflower-blue eyes pierce mine as if they're looking into my soul. I nod.

"I remember being on the *Drayant* as if it was yesterday."

Oh my God. She was on this vessel? The very same vessel where I've lain naked on the floor? Is it possible her nude body sat on the same kitchen counter I've been perching on? Ewww.

And… she's smiling. Fondly. As if these were the best days of her life.

"When I look back on those days, I'm filled with so many emotions."

Disgust? Anger? Regret at the road not traveled?

"It was hard at first. I imagine you're in the hard part, right?"

I nod. "Yes, but I imagine Voxx has already told you that."

"Your Sir and I haven't spoken since before you arrived on board except to arrange this comm."

My arrival? What a nice euphemism. How about my kidnap? My abduction?

"I cried. A lot," she continued. "I fought and ran and sassed. And I was punished. If I'm not mistaken, I see red rimming your eyes. Shall I assume you've been punished recently?"

"Yes." Why the fuck did I make this call? Jennifer's been brainwashed. That's obvious.

"I was thrilled when your Sir called and said you wanted to speak with me because I have two things I want to tell you.

The first is that I'm happy. Very happy. Inordinately happy with my life here on Zinn.

"My Master treats me well. We have fun together, we laugh together, and we raised a wonderful son together. And I have bliss in the bedroom. And in the garden. And in our hovercar. And on the kitchen counter. I love that—it reminds me of the ship." Her smile broadens.

Oh yuck. I want to hurl thinking of her naked bottom where my naked bottom has been.

"Don't worry." She laughs. "I'm sure they've washed it since then. The second thing I want to tell you is what I wish someone had told me when I was in your place. You have eleven more days. You have to live through those eleven days to get to your Choosing Day.

"I'm sure Voxx told you about that. It's written in stone. You absolutely get to choose. That's not a trick. If you want to go home, he will take you. A member of a secret American government commission will validate your choice. So don't worry about that."

Yikes, my worries hadn't even gotten that far, but they should have. I should have assumed Voxx wouldn't honor his end of the bargain and I'd only get the illusion of choice.

"So here's the advice I wish I'd had. You only have two choices: live through the next eleven days with hatred in your heart, resenting everything your Sir says and does to you. Feeling guilty for the pleasure he gives you… he does give you pleasure doesn't he, Victoria?"

That wasn't a rhetorical question? She's really asking the woman her son abducted if he gives me sexual pleasure?

"Sorry, I've been on Zinn a long time. I realize that was a horrible question to ask someone I've just met. Never mind.

So you can spend the next eleven days in agony and resentment, or you can shrug your shoulders and go with it.

"You can allow yourself to adhere to the rules, follow his orders, and immerse yourself in whatever physical bliss he provides. Either way, you'll get to Choosing Day at the same time. One way you've had eleven days of misery, the other you've had a more tolerable experience. Maybe even pleasurable.

"I hope you select the latter, Victoria. It's obvious what choice I made on Choosing Day, but that's not for everyone. I hope you allow the next few days to be more enjoyable. I hope you quit fighting the experience. Did you have other questions?"

I shake my head, feeling sorry for her. She's obviously fallen for her abuser.

"One more thing," she holds up a finger. "I'd be happy to have you for a daughter-in-law if you choose to come back to Zinn with Voxx."

The comm flickers off.

I scrub my face with my hands. She's crazy, no doubt about it. I mean, I guess not completely crazy. There are plenty of people all over the world in alternative lifestyles. Avery, my best friend from high school, is collared by her boyfriend. I didn't quite understand it, but I respect her right to choose.

Me, on this spaceship right now with the purple asshole? No. That's completely different. I had no choice. He fucking abducted me.

And just because I have amazing hour-long orgasms with him doesn't make this whole situation right. But Jennifer was correct on one count, I can't keep fighting it. Fighting hurts, it earns me punishment, and it is futile. I decide to go with the flow.

From this moment on, I'll comply.

I remove the dress, fold it neatly, lay it on the foot of the bed, then leave the bedroom. Voxx is in his captain's chair, staring into space. I settle next to him in Kneeling pose and stargaze with him while he absently strokes my head.

"Was the talk with my mother helpful?"

"Yes, Sir."

"I'm glad. I want your time here to be as easy and pleasant as possible."

"I know that." It felt disingenuous when I said it, but I realize it's true. I believe he does want my time here to be pleasurable. If I'd grown up on Zinn, this would be normal and the way he treats me would be deemed generous and nice.

When you're raised a certain way, what you see, everything you know is normal. You're swimming in your culture and don't see how different it is from other possibilities. That old saying, 'a fish doesn't know it swims in water' is true. He doesn't understand how crazy this is.

In Voxx's world, he's been nothing but nice. He's said he'd be considered lenient. This afternoon's punishment could have sucked way worse than it did.

He lifts me up and pulls me onto his lap. The square stuffed chair is wide with high, upholstered arms. The small of my back rests against one arm and my hip slides next to his naked cock. He presses my head against his chest. I melt into him. I'm tired of fighting. I'm tired of battling him, this situation, my sexual responses—all of it.

"Want to talk?"

"Mmm," I answer noncommittally.

His hand strokes my arm and we both watch the stars.

"Where are we?" Stupid question. I won't understand his answer anyway.

"Circling halfway between Earth and Zinn. It makes it easier on Choosing Day."

I nod, feeling as if a thousand-pound weight was lifted from my head. I can just be, just allow, not have to fight every second of every day.

"I haven't given up, Sir. Don't get your hopes up. I'm just... not going to fight anymore."

"Thank the Gods. I don't enjoy punishing you," his deep, masculine voice sounds relieved.

I lie with my head on his massive pec, looking out the window. Glancing at him, I can appreciate his masculine beauty. I don't have to fight the attraction anymore either.

On my deathbed, when I think of these two weeks, I'll just refer to it as my little walk on the wild side. Well, I won't refer to it at all because I won't remember a moment of it. I wonder how I'll explain to myself my sudden attraction to riding crops, nipple clamps, and beef stroganoff.

"I read about the Earth technique of red, yellow, and green. We're going to use it, starting immediately. If there's something you can't stand, I want you to say 'red'. I won't force anything on you that's red. I don't want you worrying that I'm going to whip you. I didn't like the fear in your eyes."

"Thanks." I stroke his cheek with the back of my hand. "That would help."

Ever the opportunist, he snakes his hand between my legs and slips a finger inside me.

"Tell me if this is red," he says, his voice huskier than it was a moment ago.

I wiggle and open myself to give him better access. "Not yet."

"Now?" He quirks a questioning eyebrow as he adds a second finger.

"Nope."

His thrusts are slow and steady; I hear slippery sounds from between my legs. He opens me even wider with a third finger. "How about now?"

"Can't say I'm quite to red yet, Sir," I say as I lay on my back on his lap and open my knees wider.

"Make yourself come, Victoria. Whenever you want."

I'm splayed open and safe in his arms. My fingers circle my clit and I'm so relaxed and happy I know I'll be able to come quickly.

"No, Sir. I don't want to come whenever I want. I want you to tell me."

He smiles and bends to bite my shoulder—I think he does this so I can't see his smile.

"Tell me when you're close," his voice is deep and low.

"Sir," I whisper in his ear.

"Mmm?"

"Do the thing. The thing you…" He presses his thumb into my ass part-way, and I suck in a sharp, surprised breath. "Yeah. I'm close."

"More, Victoria?"

I nod.

"Oh. Please, Sir, may I come."

He slows his fingers and presses a tiny bit farther with his thumb. "Wait."

It's heaven and hell. I'm so close to coming it's all I can do to keep from flying apart. But hanging on the edge of the scimitar's blade, a millimeter from release, is delicious.

Deep groans escape my mouth and I curl my knees toward my head as I ready myself for an explosive orgasm. My thighs are already quivering when he says, "Now," with all the force of a Five-Star General.

I splinter apart on his command. My heart thuds, a deep-throated scream rips from my mouth, and every muscle in my body spasms in release.

A moment later I'm in his arms like a bride over the threshold, my arms are around his neck and all the lights in the ship are off so we can see every star scattered in the sky.

He's kissing my forehead and cheeks and nose and eyelids. He's tender and sweet and all the things I've ever dreamed of having in a man. And he's not human, and he's purple, and this is time-limited, and I don't care.

"I don't fucking care," I mumble, then kiss him back.

Later that night when we're in bed he offers me my ten minutes.

I feel like Mata-Hari, some super-sneaky double agent, but I have to keep trying to get back to Earth before the end of the Quest.

"I still want to know, Sir. Why is this so important to you?"

He holds my gaze in his, brushes his knuckles down my cheek, and launches. "I watched my parents my whole life. What they had as a couple, what we had as a family, was normal. Well, it was normal to me. And it was wonderful.

"I always felt loved—cherished by them. When things are good, you want to grow up and have it for yourself. I knew there was a scarcity of females on my planet. I knew about the lottery, but I never gave it much thought until I made a friend from school when I was twelve.

"Manu and his father invited me for a sleepover. He was genetically conceived, as most Zinns are. Usually, a male who has aged out of the lottery arranges for a son through artificial means. They have a family, just without females in the house.

"That night was… eye-opening. And sad. I had nightmares about it for years. Nothing terrible happened. It was just… barren. No female around. No feminine energy. The house itself lacked a female's touch. Manu and his father seemed harsher somehow. Everything seemed utilitarian and lifeless.

"Males and females were meant to mate. It's a sad fact of nature that although we cleaned up our planet's pollution, the damage it did to our DNA reduced our ability to produce female children to a ten percent ratio.

"I want the love of a female, like my father has. I want to shower a female with my love. I did everything right all my life to ensure I qualified for the lottery. I've waited for this opportunity since childhood. I've read every book ever written to make certain this would succeed.

"I want this to work, Victoria. It's the most important thing in my world. Not just for me but for you. I like you and respect you. I admire everything I know about you. I want to make you happy. I want to please you."

His words were so poignant, but also crazy. For a moment I say nothing. Why argue? But I have to get him to see that he makes no sense.

"I know we come from different cultures, Voxx, but the way you've treated me since I've been on board, how can you think this would please me?"

"I don't pleasure you in bed?"

"Of course you do, but making me lie on my face on the floor in the Down position? Not just that, all the positions? Licking your fingers? Eating out of your hand? How could you think that would please me or forge a relationship?"

He leans closer to inspect me. "The books promise results. I've followed their advice. They say you'll learn to appreciate my dominance, to find the joy in submitting. I've done everything right."

"That may be what the books recommend, Voxx, but so far it's not working."

I know we've exceeded our time limit. He snugs next to me and kisses my head until I fall asleep.

Day Four

Voxx

I don't know whether it was her conversation with my mother or our ten minutes of truth, but something shifted. Whatever happened demolished some barriers between us.

She cuddled up to me under the covers, and even when she woke up this morning, she didn't scurry to the edge of the bed; she stayed close.

Before my voyage, my father warned me of many things: not to be too rough, to make certain to attend to her sexual pleasure, but these were all discussions we'd had many times. Right before I boarded the *Drayant,* he warned me of something new.

"You're a good male, Voxx. I'm proud to call you my son. I would have never told you this if you hadn't won the lottery, but you need to hear it before you go. You can be soft, Voxx. You were too soft training Argyle and Socks when we got them as puppies. You can be too soft with the males you supervise. Keep the balance with this female, Voxx. It will only work back on Zinn if you stay firm with her.

"My friend, Lazz, from work was too soft with his female. He compromised many times in order for her to choose Zinn on Choosing Day. Their relationship is full of strife and clashes. He didn't choose well, his mate fights him for dominance. It's a terrible match.

"You have to maintain command, son. Be clever, it's a razor's edge to walk, but you have to allow her to feel all the caring you have for her while always maintaining your dominance."

This was my own father's advice. It's congruent with every book I read. Victoria told me my methods are failing, but how could all the books be wrong? Only 3% of Earth females go back home on Choosing Day. No matter what Victoria said last night, I need to stay the course.

I need to remain the dominant with her.

"Kneel."

"Where, Sir?"

"Right here in bed."

"Yes, Sir. With alacrity." She's in her position, in correct form in a moment. How could I not be proud of her?

"Your breasts are perfect."

"Thank you, Sir." Her eyes dip shyly to the bed.

"Tomorrow you'll begin lessons on how to pleasure me."

"Yes, Sir."

"Today I learn more about you."

"Yes, Sir." She steals an inquisitive glance at me, then studies the mattress again.

I've waited all my life for this opportunity. It wasn't until two months ago that I won the lottery. Since then, thirty-three years of anticipation came together in a hurry. Now that I have my own female, sitting at the ready inches from me, it's taking every ounce of strength not to rut her like a wild beast.

I won't be able to last more than one additional day. I've been following the books' instructions on this, too. No penetration until Day Six. I'll continue to follow the plan.

"We'll take a shower together and then you'll cook breakfast."

"Yes, Sir."

I had every intention of getting into the shower with her immediately, but my mouth orders, "Present," before I'm aware I'm talking.

She hurries off the bed to lie on the floor when I stop her.

"Bed," I say as I stand.

She lies on the bed, arms above her head, legs spread wide for me.

"Wider," I bark. After she spreads her legs as far as they'll go, I grab her ankles and open her even wider for my enjoyment. I memorize every pink fold.

"Tell me what you've enjoyed about our sex-play since you've been on board. I'll watch as you moisten." I sit, one bent knee propped on the bed, the other foot on the floor.

She gnaws on her bottom lip, probably deciding what she wants to share.

"The truth, Victoria. I'll see the proof of your words displayed down below."

"I like looking at your cock, Sir. It's amazing. I like the way you touch my nipples. Your mouth, your teeth on them is wonderful."

When she pauses I grab her hand from above her head and place it between her legs. "Feel that?" my voice is low, "you're going to keep talking until you drip onto the sheets. Use those wonderful words of yours, barrister. Paint a verbal picture for me." I tug her hand back above her head.

"Yes, Sir." She closes her eyes and launches. "The way you look at me sometimes, like you want to pounce on me, turns me on. It makes me feel beautiful."

"Good girl, Victoria. That's what I want." I drop a kiss on her lips and tell her, "I'm glad I make you feel beautiful, but it's not hard work, you *are* beautiful."

"And, Sir… when you call me 'good girl' my clit twinges every single time."

"Good girl." I bend to nip her inner thigh, she smells divine.

"And that, Sir. That just gave me a hard zing of pleasure right to my clit. Which would love your tongue on it right this minute, Sir."

"I am the dominant in this relationship, *zara*. I do not take direction well." Grabbing the crop from where it was still sitting on the nightstand, I gently flick her clit with the square flap of leather. She sucks air in through her teeth, pressing her head against the pillows for a moment.

"Describe that for me."

"It surprised me. I thought it was pain for a moment, but it was delicious."

I grasp her hand and press her middle finger into her core. "You're not wet enough, *zara*. The sheets aren't soaked with your cream." I put her hand back above her head.

"I love it when you tell me not to come. It's a pain/pleasure package. I'm learning my own responses better. And the G-spot. When you press there, it's powerful."

"There's a glistening stream dripping down your slit, Victoria, but it hasn't reached the bed. Tell me the most embarrassing thing right this moment. Don't think, just tell me."

"I loved your finger in my ass," she says without hesitation.

"More," I urge, my voice soft.

"It made everything more intense. It made me feel full and tight and… mastered. And I hate that I liked it, but I did."

"Get on your hands and knees. Face the back wall," I bark. She flips over, complying instantly. "Good girl. Put your cheek on the bed, your ass in the air."

Even though her position is perfectly fine and so sexy I want to take her right this moment, I grab the crop and press it from under her hip bone to urge her ass even higher. "That's right, Victoria. I'm the dominant, but I will comply if you ask me right now. Tell me what you want me to do to that fine-looking ass of yours."

"Fuck it. Fuck my ass." She's breathless and dripping wet for me.

"No fucking today. What else could I do for you?"

"Penetrate me, please, Sir."

I bend over and whisper in her ear. "My finger or this riding crop, Victoria?"

Her answer is a whisper so quiet I can't hear her.

"Tell me immediately or you'll get nothing up this pretty little ass." I swat one cheek.

"The riding crop, Sir." I heard her this time, but I want to hear it louder. I want her to own her desires.

"Louder."

"The riding crop, Sir."

"What should I do with the riding crop, little Victoria?"

"Fuck my ass with the riding crop, Sir."

"I think 'please' would be in order," I scold. There's a smile on my face which she can't see.

She's dripping wet, wiggling her ass in the air as she says loud and clear, "Sir, I would love it if you would put the riding crop in my ass. Please, Sir."

"As you wish."

I press three fingers into her core, and she moans in pleasure.

"You like this, pretty Victoria?"

"Yes, Sir. Thank you, Sir."

I remove my fingers, ride the crop handle along her slit until it's slick with her juices, then penetrate her core with it.

"Like that, Victoria?"

"Umm, yes, Sir."

"Ready?"

"Yes, Sir. Please."

Pulling the crop out of her core, I press it against her back hole. Returning two fingers to her pussy, I fill her up, then press into her backside with the handle of the crop.

"Oh, Sir. So good."

"Tell me if it's too much. Say the word red. Otherwise, your Sir is going to fuck you like this until you come."

I press fingers and crop in unison, then alternate, discovering the exact rhythm and depth she desires.

"Oh, so good, Sir."

"Touch yourself, *zara*. You'll need permission to come."

"Yes, Sir."

Less than five seconds later, "Close, Sir."

"Wait."

"Trouble." she's struggling to maintain.

"Wait," I put steel into my voice.

"Please. Sir."

"Come for me."

Her inner walls spasm around my fingers as I hear loud, guttural moans interspersed with high, keening shrieks. It goes on for a minute or more until her legs quiver uncontrollably. I throw the crop on the floor, climb next to her, press her to the bed, and throw an arm and a leg over her.

"Oh my God," she says as she nestles against me.

Victoria

I know it cheapens the phrase to say that the sex was life-altering, but it was. I'm still spasming in aftershocks as I cuddle next to Voxx. He played my body like a musical instrument. And my mind. That whole 'tell me what turns you on' exchange got me out of my head which allowed my body to rise to greater heights of pleasure.

I can't imagine saying things like that to another living soul, but I said them to him. And he doesn't seem scandalized.

As if in answer to my unspoken question, he says, "You were magnificent, *zara*. Watching you allow yourself to experience all that pleasure. It was a gift you gave me. It delights me to see you explore your boundaries."

"Really, that didn't repulse you?"

"Repulse?"

He lifts my chin with a finger so I'm looking at him. "You wonder if your sexual responses repulse me? There are few women on my planet. Females are to be cherished. Since adolescence, every male's only dream is to find a female to mate.

"We study how to sexually pleasure them and pray to be lucky enough to meet our own female one day. I would do anything to make you happy. What happens in this bed is only between us. Anything that gives you pleasure is my honor to provide. I channel my dominant urges into making you explore your sexual boundaries."

He kisses me gently, carries me into the shower and lathers me, then rinses, then lathers again.

"What does *zara* mean," I ask as warm water sluices down my head and over my face.

"Hands on the back wall, butt out."

I do as I'm told.

"It's a term of endearment on Zinn."

"What exactly does it mean?"

"What does 'honey', or 'precious' mean on Earth? It's a pet name."

"Oh." My big, dominant Zinn is now calling me by a pet name—flattering. "Haven't we been in here more than ten minutes? The water's still warm."

"I ordered it to override instructions."

"You manipulated me the other day," I say in mock disgust.

"Shouldn't you end your sentence with Sir?"

"You tricked me the other day, Sir."

"Butt farther back," he orders, then toes my feet as far apart as the small metal-walled shower will allow. I'm glad my hands are on the wall or I'd lose my balance.

His soapy fingers slide back-and-forth along my slit. This shuts me up and focuses my concentration.

"I'm going to clean my *zara* very well," he breathes into my ear. I feel his cock bob against my backside as he steps closer and 'cleans' me from the front giving such ample attention to my clit that I can barely keep my knees from buckling.

"Am I clean yet, Sir?"

"Hardly."

One soapy finger nudges at my back hole.

"Relax, *zara*." I pay attention to the pressure, the tiny zap of pain, and then the pleasure of penetration. "Any complaints?"

"None, Sir."

A second finger knocks at my backdoor. A bolt of fear snakes through me, this will be bigger than the crop.

"Take a breath."

I do, and the finger finds its way inside. Another moment of pressure and then that snug feeling of fullness that tells my brain I'm a possession—*his* possession.

"What a very good girl you are, *zara*."

"Thank you, Sir."

His fingers begin a rhythm and my hips dance to it. He reaches around me and plucks each nipple in turn. I slide into a haze of lust, focused only on my sensitive peeks and what's going on behind me.

"Does this feel good?"

"Yes, Sir."

"Tell me."

"Sir, that feels wonderful."

"What feels wonderful?"

"That. Sir."

"Tell me what I'm doing."

I take a deep breath and let it all out in a quick gush. "Your fingers pumping in my ass feel amazing, Sir. I feel your cock bobbing against me and hear your panting and my own and it is incendiary, Sir. The fullness makes me feel owned by you, Sir."

Shit, I really shouldn't have said that last part. I need to keep some secrets. Of course, he'll pounce on that.

"And do you like feeling owned, *zara*?"

I should hesitate, I know. I shouldn't admit it, but I do. With alacrity. "I like it, Sir."

"Good girl. Play with yourself. Beg me to come."

A minute later, I'm begging.

Two minutes later, he gives permission.

Three minutes later I sag against his wet chest in a heap of spent muscles and quivering thighs.

Four minutes later he's toweling me dry and kissing me.

"Cook me breakfast," he orders. I guess we're both going commando today.

He teaches me how to cook *chernoy*, his favorite breakfast. He's infinitely patient, which is good because I'm infinitely incompetent. I can't remember the names of half the ingredients or half the kitchen tools. Under his tutelage, the result isn't half bad.

"You can have an hour alone, Victoria. I want you kneeling at my side in sixty minutes."

The clock on the computer screen reads out in both Earth and Zinn minutes. I make note of the time and clean the galley, then grab the reader and go to the bedroom.

Whoops, I picked up his reader by mistake. I peek out the door and see he's busy in his captain's seat. He's not going to notice the mix-up. I wonder what he keeps on it.

It's filled with books about how to manage the Quest. He told me Zinns have to be fluent in English to qualify for the lottery, so I'm not too surprised I'm able to read almost every book he has on here.

I keep my eye on the clock and skim several of the manuals. He wasn't lying. They all delineate, in minute detail, how to dominate Earth females. They're thorough, I'll give them that. And Voxx has tried his damnedest to follow their instructions.

The female should not be allowed to awaken on your ship alone. This would disturb and frighten her. Be reassuring as you use the tools you've brought on your Quest to bring her to orgasm over and over. This will provide a reassuring and pleasant introduction to you.

"Not exactly," I whisper to the empty room.

In another book:

Utilize the positions delineated in chapter two to help her succumb to her submissive nature. Even if the female protests, it is her way of letting you know she isn't ready to accept your dominance. If this occurs, redouble your efforts to assert your mastery.

I skip back to chapter two to take a gander at other outrageous positions shown in pictures. These are terrible, although nothing is worse than Down.

In a third book:

Don't demonstrate any soft or loving emotions. This will only serve to confuse your female. Developing the loving relationship that is your end goal can only occur after dominance has been established.

It's hard to hate him for what he's done when he's following his instruction manuals to the letter.

With only minutes left to return to Voxx's side, I leave his reader at his bedside to retain plausible deniability.

I slide into the perfect Kneeling position at his side with one minute to spare.

"Here." He points a few inches in front of me with the crop. The crop. Fuck, it smells like me. I try to hide my embarrassment, but my cheeks burn.

I move into position and say nothing more than, "Yes, Sir."

"You can get more comfortable if you wish to rest your head on my knee."

I make certain he can't see my contented smile as I follow his instructions. He turns on music and pets my head. It's the first Zinnian music I've heard, other than the porno music from the vids I watched. Funny, they resembled the boom chicka boom of porno back on Earth.

These melodies are rhythmic and lilting and lull me into a serene place. I try not to think at all because when I do I always fall into self-loathing about how easily I became Voxx's little sex toy.

A visual montage of pictures flashes through my head. Me in the shower, me with a riding crop up my ass. Oh, dear God, did I really beg for that an hour ago? Me splayed out on the bed and on the floor with my legs so wide he could see my cream drip down my folds. I grind my molars together to silence a groan of self-loathing.

I asked him if I repulsed him. The truth of the matter is that I repulse myself. I'm a ho. A horny, sex-crazed ho. And one other thing I'm certain of—I'm incapable of stopping until Choosing Day when he deposits me back on Earth.

There's one saving grace. He'll wipe my mind and I won't remember the sexual bliss we shared. Maybe, if I'm very lucky, he won't have spoiled me for any other male in the future. Because if he didn't wipe my mind, I know as certainly as Earth's sky is blue, that no male would ever hold a candle to Voxx in bed. Ever.

"I'd like to show you my planet."

Every muscle in my body tightens at his quiet suggestion. He told me we were circling halfway between his planet and mine. If I set foot on Zinn does that nullify the contract? Do I become a Zinnian bride without benefit of a verbal agreement? Do I become his chattel?

"What does that mean, Sir? Sorry. I'm not ready to—"

"Don't worry, little Earther, I was going to show you vids. Although I could take you to Zinn. I'd still bring you back to Earth on Choosing Day if that's what you want."

Slumping back onto his thigh, I huff out a relieved breath.

"I'd like to see vids of your planet, Sir."

I'm still not quite certain how, but his nervous system must sync with the ship because he simply thinks something and the ship responds. The windows on the bridge play pictures of Zinn. This vid must have been produced by the "Welcome to Zinn for New Earth Brides Committee," because it's a hard sell for the planet.

A male speaking perfect English begins a mellifluous voiceover as the screens show a spinning planet very much like Earth, although everything has purple tones instead of blue. It appears that if the sky is purple, the water down below reflects that color as well.

The planet is breathtaking. There's lavender sky and water, green continents that are startling because it's a reflex reaction to expect continents to be shaped like ours and they're so different.

The vid explains some of their geopolitics. Zinns have a one-world government. It was the only way they curbed their raging pollution and military overspending to get a handle on saving their planet.

The vid brags about the complete lack of homelessness, the absence of any intraplantary wars over the last two centuries, and the prosperity that reigns over their planet.

"We have made every effort to accommodate the presence of our valued Earth females," the voiceover concludes. "From an abundance of Earth canines and felines to edible livestock, to heirloom vegetables we've imported from your planet, we try to make your stay as comfortable as possible.

"For those of you with strong religious beliefs, every Zinnian male has agreed to be trained in your ideology and mated in your faith should you request it. Our physicians are highly skilled in fertility and obstetrical concerns. Should you wish, we have trained counselors assigned to each of you to help you adjust as quickly and painlessly as possible to your new way of life.

"Once you step foot upon Zinn soil, you become a full citizen of our planet. Rest assured, any children you produce will be afforded the full rights of Zinn citizenship as well. We welcome you to Zinn and hope to meet you on Choosing Day."

Voxx is still petting my hair when the vid ends. I have to admit, one of the things I like about him is that when we're not in the bedroom—or the shower or the bridge—he allows me time to think.

"Your planet is beautiful," I say on a sigh.

"It is," he says matter-of-factly without a hint of boastfulness.

"How much of it is true?"

"What do you mean?"

"It's obviously a puff piece. It's a travelogue designed to entice us Earth brides to be Zinnian Stepford wives. How much is smoke?"

"Smoke?"

"You're not familiar with the expression 'blowing smoke up your ass'?" I turn to look at him.

"It's all true. The planet looks exactly as you observed. You would become a full citizen if you choose Zinn on Choosing Day."

"Come on, Sir. No homelessness? No war? No poverty?" He must think I'm an idiot, those things just aren't possible.

"I know you still think I'm a purple asshole, Victoria. You say it in your sleep. I may well be, but I don't lie. I'd suggest you ask my mother, but I get the impression you don't hold her in high regard."

I don't deny it; my gaze flies from his.

"Let's make dinner. My mother sent a care package with specific food she says you will appreciate along with recipes in case you don't have them committed to memory. She's had me make them with her once a year since I was eighteen in preparation for this night. Come with me."

He escorts me into the bedroom, opens a dresser drawer, and pulls out a pretty pink dress he picked out for me. I always thought pink went well with my complexion, but I guess he knew that. He's been Facebook stalking me for years.

"Call me when you're dressed." Voxx leaves me in blissful privacy.

Clothes! It almost feels awkward when I put on the dress. It's useless to twirl in front of the single mirror in the ship; it's over the sink in the bathroom and only reflects from my boobs up. I feel such relief wearing something—anything. Maybe this cloak of civility will help me reject his sexual advances tonight.

"I'm dressed, Sir," I call when I've run out of reasons to have more alone time.

"Sit." He enters, grabs a brush from the dresser, and points to the foot of the bed. Sitting next to me, he nudges his hip next to mine. "Close your eyes."

I obey. He gathers my long hair in one hand and brushes it with the other. The words 'better than sex' float through my brain. I moan in pleasure.

"This collar mars your beauty, *zara*. I want to take it off, but I need to trust you won't break any rules in the middle of the night." He dips his head to my ear, "Can I trust you?"

"I'm here for the next ten days, Sir. I know resistance is futile."

"I know that reference, Victoria. I'm not the Borg."

"Drat, I thought I could slip that one by you, Sir," my voice is cheery, and I brush my hand on his thigh to lighten the mood.

When I used to fantasize about being married, when I was young and didn't know about sex, I pictured this. A man gently brushing my hair. I love nothing more than this. Well, I guess after the last few days I've discovered a couple things I love more than this. But this is one of the most luxurious, pampered feelings in the world—in the universe.

It's been days since I did anything other than finger-comb my hair, but he's managing the process with no pain. He's patient and skilled and works the brush through it until all the tangles are gone. Then he brushes from scalp to ends. I want to melt into the bed, but I stay erect, let my eyelids flutter closed, and allow myself to breathe deep and relax.

"You like that?" His warm breath rustles next to my ear. "This feels good?"

"Mmm." I nod.

"This almost put you to sleep. Next time, I'll do it at bedtime."

Next time? A happy childlike part of me sits up inside and claps, taking notice of his promise. "That would be amazing, Sir."

"I've changed the rules for tonight. You may call me Voxx if you like. There will be no positions tonight either. And no orders. But no profanity, no hitting, and no escape attempts."

"Yes, Sir." Oops. "Voxx."

He gives me a calm, close-lipped smile, his silver gaze bathes me in warmth, like a visual caress.

Tonight is going to be different.

Once he pulls all the food out of storage, I see we'll be celebrating Thanksgiving. Not a Zinn Thanksgiving, but a real Thanksgiving from Earth. Was it coming up? It was late October when he abducted me, but I won't complain.

The Zinns must have brought some of the best Earth food to their planet because laid out on the counter is a real turkey, as well as the fixings for stuffing, gravy, and pumpkin pie.

"I was a mac and cheese girl, Voxx. I'm not much of a cook." I shrug.

"Then I'll teach you," he says as he gets to work. He's wearing black slacks and a thin, black sweater that hugs his muscles. It goes well with his lavender skin and white hair. The contrast makes him look even sexier, which I didn't think was possible.

It's ironic to see the purple alien guy cooking traditional Thanksgiving dinner like a champ, and me not knowing how to do more than open the container of cranberries. He's very precise as he explains all the ins and outs of the meal prep.

"My mother said it's very important to thicken the gravy with this." He holds up a container. "You have to add it to the turkey drippings when they're cool, or you'll get lumps."

"You prepared for this night for years?"

"Don't you realize how important this is?" His silver gaze lasers into mine. "I…" He quiets, his eyes looking at the ceiling as if he's deep in thought, like this is the most important thing he's said in decades. "I don't just want a mate, Victoria. You're not a random choice. I didn't pick up the first available Earth female I saw.

"I picked you. I want you. I realize I know far more about you than I should. But I appreciate everything I know. Nothing is more important to me than you. Mom said you'd feel comforted by this meal. I want it to be special and just the way you like it."

He instructs me on how to put the turkey in the hot box, then teaches me every step of making stuffing.

"We're making pie crust from scratch?" I ask incredulously as he pulls out flour. Even my mom, who occasionally sews her own clothes and cans homemade strawberry jam, has never made her own pie crust.

"I'm told I make mine light and flaky," he says with a hint of pride.

I giggle. Big, strong purple asshole is standing in his black slacks and shirt dusted with flour. Two hours ago he was fucking me with a riding crop and ordering me to call him Sir.

Now he's instructing me on the finer points of making the perfect crust. It's such a juxtaposition of incongruity my mind's having trouble wrapping around it.

I can't stop laughing. Maybe it's that for the first time in three days I'm not in fear. For this moment at least, I'm not worrying that he'll hurt me or make me do something I don't want.

Picking up a pinch of flour, he flicks it at me. I'm sure it's spattered all over my face, just as it is on the bodice of my pink dress.

"You got me dirty!" I grab a handful of the flour on the counter and poof it at him. Now there's a white cloud on his chest. My heart thuds when I realize I was playing with him and he's a mammoth purple alien from Zinn who'll punish me for stepping over the line.

My eyes widen as I wait for retaliation.

"You're going to pay for that, Victoria."

Oh, no. But when I glance at him, he's grinning. His face has lost all its harshness. He looks handsome. He stares at me for a moment, his close-mouthed grin slashing wider.

"I know exactly how you're going to pay, *zara*—after the pie is in the hot box. Come back over here," he commands.

Positioning himself behind me, he places his hands around me and instructs me on how to properly knead dough. He keeps brushing flour off my breasts, taking care to remove all flour molecules from my front.

"Now we've overworked the dough; we'll have to start again," he says in mock irritation. "Your dress is going to get ruined, you'll have to take it off."

I reach to the hem to pull the dress up, but he grabs one hand. "I said no orders tonight. Only take it off if you want to." His eyes spark with desire.

I bend to grasp the hem, but he stops me with his words. "If I *were* giving orders, though, I would tell you to do it slowly, as if you were enticing a lover. I would never order you to do that, though. Not tonight."

I pierce him with what I hope is my sexiest smile, bend my knees, and grasp the hem of my pink dress between thumbs and forefingers. Shimmying the fabric up my thighs, I pause and lick my lips as slowly as possible. Heat flares along my veins as I see his appreciative response, his gaze focused on my every action.

He didn't provide me with panties, so when my hem approaches my waist, his stare rivets at the triangle of brown hair at my mound.

"If I was giving orders, I'd tell you to widen your stance," his voice is a husky murmur, his eyes flick from the apex of my thighs, to my breasts, and back.

I stand still, feeling cocky and in control. Licking my lips again, I feign taking a moment to decide, then I move one foot an inch to the right, then the other an inch to the left. I open my legs more slowly than I could have imagined, while my attention focuses first on the hot lust displayed on his face, and then to the growing size of his package. I love this feeling of control.

Turning away from him, I reopen my stance and bend down, one vertebra at a time until my palms touch the floor. I close my mind to the image projected inside my head of what Voxx must be seeing. I imagine he's observing every detail of my ass and intimate, pink folds under the bright galley lights. I'm splayed open to him, ass thrust back, legs open as wide as possible.

As embarrassing as the image in my head looks to me, the sharp intake of his breath is proof he's enjoying the show.

"You're beautiful."

After I let the loose dress slide over my head and pool on the floor, I expose my breasts through the keyhole of my legs. I hear a strangled noise behind me.

"If I were in charge right now, two fingers would be pressed inside you and my thumb would be in your ass. Of course, I'd never force you to accept such behavior."

"I'd never encourage such behavior, Voxx. Not unless I was dripping wet. Come see if I am." Equal measures of lust and shame slice through me. I can't go an hour without wanting this male.

He bridges the distance between us and his hand slips between my legs. Two fingers slide along my channel, already slick with my desire. His thumb rests on my private hole.

"Too bad you're not wet, *zara*. You'd need plenty of stimulation to be wet enough for me to slip inside you."

With every pass his hand makes, his fingertips kiss my sensitive bud.

"If I were in charge, I'd tell you Wall. Your hands on the wall would keep you from falling over in this pose."

The blood has been pooling in my head so long I'm lightheaded, so I move to the wall, place my hands upon it and bend as low as I can. One second later Voxx's left hand returns to the same position and his right plucks my clit. My hips move back seeking more of his touch.

"Please, Voxx." I'm panting, desperate, needing him inside me.

"Please what?"

"Make me come."

His fingers slide inside me at the same moment his thumb enters me from behind. Bliss. I reach down and circle my clit and come almost immediately. I feel spent and limp and still horny at the same time.

I don't know how long he plans to suspend the rules. I need to ask him something now, even as I'm panting and spiraling down from my sex-induced high.

"Why won't you fuck me, Voxx?" I reach behind and grab his cock through the fabric of his messy black pants.

"There are reasons, *zara*. Tomorrow you learn my body. The day after you'll feel my cock inside you. For a female who thinks I'm a purple asshole, are you certain you want this inside you?"

He grabs my hip bones and presses his rigid length against me so hard I feel every rocklike inch of him.

"Yes." I say before I know the word is out of my mouth. Yep, I'm a ho.

Voxx

I love having her kneeling at my side. I love telling her to come and seeing her burst into blissful release. I also love seeing her playful side. And just now, when she initiated our sexplay, that was the best of all. It's one thing for her to comply, it's quite another for her to instigate it.

While she's taking another shower, I make her a present with the 3-D printer. I'll give it to her before dinner. We have hours before the meal is ready.

"I'm out of the shower," she calls from the bedroom. "What did you want me to wear? The pink dress is filthy."

"I told you I wanted to learn you today," I say as I walk into the bedroom. "No clothes."

She looks at me expectantly, a hint of excitement in her eyes. "I promised I'd be Voxx for the rest of the day, but do you want Voxx or Sir to join you in bed?" Whatever will make her more comfortable.

She reflects for a long moment. I've discovered whenever she does that she gets in her own way. "I'm going to be Sir, unless you object right now."

"No objections, Sir."

She likes my dominance. It's how things work best.

"Present." She gets into position on her back, hands over her head, legs spread.

"Lovely." I sit on the bed next to her and stroke her head. This always relaxes her. My hands soon stray to her torso where they roam from waist to neck, taking extra time on her breasts.

"Yesterday I explored your G-spot. Today I want to find your other spots."

"Other spots?"

"I've kept abreast of research on your Internet. There are thunk spots and the A-zone. I want to discover all the uncharted territory inside you so I can provide greater pleasure."

"I can't imagine more pleasure, Sir," she sounds sincere and wholehearted.

Pressing her wrists into the bed above her head, I crush my lips to hers. "I'm going to fuck you in a few days' time. I guarantee there will be more pleasure," I grit out.

"Yes, Sir."

I kiss her for long minutes, then lavish attention on her nipples with my mouth. Only when she's dripping for me do I penetrate her with two fingers, immediately finding her G-spot and coaxing her into a full-body release.

"Thank you, Sir."

"That's right. I like when you thank me for your release. I don't want it to be a rule. I want it to come from your heart."

After she descends from her lazy bliss, I enter her again and search farther into her core to find the A-spot I read about on Earth Internet. I find the patch inside her, above the G-spot. It's sensitive and ramps her up, but doesn't give her release.

The G-spot does. She pushes my hand from between her legs after she comes down from her body's ecstasy. "Thank you, Sir. That was wonderful, but *no mas*. Too much, Sir. Too much right now. Can we find those other spots another day?"

"Good for you, Victoria. Let me know when you've had enough. Take a nap. I'll wake you for dinner."

~.~

"Wake up," I call from the other room. "I have a present for you." Entering the bedroom, I can't help but smile down at her. She looks so soft and feminine lying in the tangled sheets, her hair mussed.

"What is it, Sir?"

I've confused her with the name change. I think she's more comfortable calling me Sir than Voxx. And I think she likes me being her Sir—at least today.

"I ruined your pink dress. Here's the blue one from yesterday. You called it your Vermillion Rabbit dress as I recall."

"Vermillion Rabbit?"

"Wasn't that what you called it?"

"Ohh, Scarlett O'Hara."

"Isn't hare another name for a rabbit? Is that how I messed things up? Did I switch Vermillion for Scarlett?"

"All that time on the Internet and you still missed a few things." She teases. "Where's my present?"

"You said it needed petticoats. That took a bit of research, but I think this is what you wanted. I made it with the 3-D printer. It's called a crinoline petticoat."

I carry in a large bell-shaped stiff undergarment meant to make the dress flounce even wider around her. "These," I point to the inflexible ribs ringing the garment, "are called hoops. Get yourself dressed and surprise me in the galley," I say as I leave to finish dinner.

Victoria

My purple asshole has given me inexpressible physical bliss all day, and now he's produced an elaborate costume out of my childhood fantasy. I shouldn't be so forgiving, but I list a dozen ways he's shown me kindness since I've been onboard. Besides the dress and the petticoat, there's tonight's dinner, the phone call to his mom, brushing my hair. I could go on and on.

My snarky side wants to delineate all the dominant behavior that was out of line, but I understand it's in his culture. I consider him a purple asshole far less frequently than I think of his gorgeous silver eyes and the hands that provide me so much pleasure.

I slip into the crinoline, then pull the dress over my head. It buttons in the back, so there's no way to put it on properly without his help.

I work the knots out of my hair, but I wish it was his hand wielding the brush.

Why I care about whether he'll like what he sees, I'll never understand, but I do. I want him to glance up from the turkey and not be able to hide the appreciation in his eyes.

I have to squish the crinoline through the doorway to make my way the few steps to the galley. And lucky me, he gives me just the look I was hoping for. His face lights in a smile as he examines me from head to toe and back again.

"You look so… feminine. And beautiful. If I hadn't just made you scream in pleasure, I'd tear those clothes off of you and do it again."

He lifts me up and plops me on one of the two kitchen stools at the bar. I would have never been able to do this myself in this cumbersome dress. Going to the bathroom will be a lesson in humiliation.

"I'll serve you tonight, *zara*."

He's gorgeous as usual in his clean black shirt and pants. He's abandoned the t-shirt, though, and is wearing a silky button-down that accentuates every muscle of his torso.

He dishes up one plate with some of everything on it. *Go you, Jennifer, you taught your son right: turkey, dressing, mashed potatoes and gravy, and cranberries.* Everything you'd expect for a family Thanksgiving dinner is on my plate, and I slept through most of it while Voxx slaved away in the galley.

He pulls his chair by my side, cuts perfect bites, and feeds me. Wow, I never imagined anything like this, and it's so freaking sexy. Within a few minutes, he knows I like gravy on every bite, and I like to alternate between mashed potatoes and stuffing.

"Aren't you eating?" I ask. He's been so attentive to me it took me a moment to notice.

"I've been snacking. This meal is about you."

Perhaps I don't fully understand the dynamic. I thought I was the slave and he was the master, but I'm not going to protest. He's doting on me. I don't recall ever being the focus of anyone's attention like this before.

My parents loved me and cared for me and I wanted for nothing, but they were busy working long hours to make ends meet.

This kind of attention is new to me, but I have to say I have no objections.

And the look in his eyes, as if he wants every bite to be perfect and he hungers for me and not food? Wow!

"Everything you cooked is amazing, Voxx. I can't wait to taste the pie," I tell him as I finish the last bite on my plate.

"And the cranberries you opened—a culinary feat," he jokes.

A pang of sadness jolts through me. No, wistfulness is the right word. This moment, right now, why can't I have more of this? Why is it I can't find a man on Earth who's attentive and helpful and kind and looks at me like he can't wait to eat me up—literally?

Back on Earth I met lots of guys, had relationships with a few, but none were marriage material. Most weren't even boyfriend material. Not only would I never have wanted to spend my life—or even the next year—with them, but none of them were that excited about me, either.

And here's Voxx, he ticks a lot of the right boxes. Handsome—check. Built—check, check. Good in bed—I'd need a long row of boxes to check on this one. When he's Voxx, he's also kind and thoughtful and a good cook.

But he's only Voxx for the night. Like Cinderella at the ball, tomorrow the footmen turn into mice and the carriage turns into a pumpkin and Voxx turns into—Sir. Demanding, dreadful, disagreeable Sir. The Sir of difficult positions and high expectations and lack of empathy. The Sir whose hot glance dampens my panties. The Sir who embarrasses me by reminding me I would let him—no *beg* him—to touch me in all the right places and in all the wrong ways.

"I'll help you with the dishes, but you and I and that dress can't all fit into the galley," he offers.

"Can you help me get out of it?"

"I thought you'd never ask," a lopsided grin slashes across his face.

After tugging the dress up over my head, he pulls the crinolines down, then stows them in the tiny alcove on top of the 3-D printer.

"I have several of what you would call t-shirts, let me get you one."

When he returns a moment later with a black t-shirt, size 2X, which fits his perfect body like a glove, I've already made up my mind.

"No, thanks." I'm weak and cravenly. There's a constant argument waging in my head. A war between lust and logic. Why is it for the past four days lust is the constant winner? I want to be naked with Sir the rest of the night.

The slow, sly smile takes moments to light up his face. "A present for me Victoria?" One eyebrow rises in question. "You wish to prance around for me without benefit of clothing? I'll find a way to return your gift." He spears me with a look so hot it would turn metal to ash.

We make quick work of cleanup and retire to the bridge.

"No kneeling tonight. I want you on my lap. There's another vid I want you to watch."

He sits in his captain's chair and motions me over. There's something sexy about being naked when he's fully clothed. It accentuates the unbalanced power dynamic, which for some reason turns me on.

"Watch the stars with me."

He communicates directly with the ship because the view out the floor-to-ceiling windows morphs from what I assume is normal to magnified. It's kind of scary because a lot of the stars appear close enough to bash into us. I have to remind myself we're safe and it's an optical illusion.

He makes another adjustment and new stars come into view. "That one, *zara*. That's Zinn."

"Miss it?"

He shakes his head, pensive. "Wondering what it will be like to go home without you. To have known this," he squeezes me, "and be alone after... my life won't be the same. It's one thing to never have it. But to have it and lose it..." The far-off look in his eyes is heartbreaking.

Tough. Poor you, the bitchy voice in my head taunts him silently. I can't help but imagine though, how awful it would be to want this your whole life, find it, and come home empty-handed.

"And here," his voice lightens and the view out the windows whirls to another part of the galaxy so fast it makes my stomach lurch. "Here is Earth."

It isn't like those pretty pictures of Earth from space where it's a big blue and white and green spinning ball. No, it's so far away it's just a twinkle.

Even if I wanted to stay on Zinn, I can't imagine leaving my family and never seeing them again. And that's not gonna happen. I know what will happen on Choosing Day, and it's not going to be team purple.

He settles deeper into the padded chair and presses his knees together, then arranges me so my bottom is nestled firmly against his cock and my knees are outside his. I'm spread wide for him. I hate that this thrills me, but it does.

"We're going to watch a vid together. I've never seen it, either. My mother made it."

The vid displays on every other one of the floor-to-ceiling windows. His mom appears, smiling happily and waving. She looks younger than she did last night. She must have recorded this segment years ago.

"Hi, nameless, faceless Earth female who's lucky enough to be chosen by my son, Voxx. I picked his name, by the way. It means voice. Zinnian babies are loud and demanding by nature, natch." She winks into the camera. "I was told that Voxx had a louder, more robust cry than most. I'd wanted his name to start with a 'V' like his father's so… that's how he got his name.

"Here, you be the judge." She inserts a home movie of little Voxx—a much smaller, much purpler version—in his space-age crib demonstrating an ear-splitting cry.

"Lusty from the start, huh big guy?"

He smiles.

"From the minute I got pregnant I knew I would produce this vid, for you, nameless, faceless Earth female. My mate, Verris, has brought me so much joy, and I to him. I've wanted nothing more than my beloved son to have the bliss of winning the lottery and finding his mate.

"If you're anything like me, it's going to be a hard sell for you to make the 'right' decision on Choosing Day." She makes air quotes. "So I'm going to diligently add to this movie along the way as I watch my beautiful son grow up. And you get to come along on the ride as you watch this vid.

"I decided I'm not going to let my dear son see this until he watches it with you. When you watch this, Voxx," she looks right into the camera, "I hope it reminds you how very much your parents loves you. I've told you a million times. I hope you see through my eyes how much I've loved you from the start."

We watch little vignettes starting from his birth up to his reading the official Zinn document informing him of his acceptance into the 'brides' program as they euphemistically call it.

His finger stopped lazily circling my clit after the first minute, and he ensconced me comfortably on his lap in as non-sexual a pose as is possible for a naked girl and a huge purple male.

He's been reflexively swallowing for long minutes, trying to push down his emotions. I'm emotional, too, as I watch so many wonderful moments of his life. Every highlight was here, from report cards to school plays. I watch his sports accomplishments and defeats. Funny, they play baseball, football, and soccer on Zinn. I guess it makes sense, all the soccer moms come from Earth.

I listen to some pep talks his father gave him when he was struggling. Although he's had no time on camera, Verris is kind and loving to his son and wife. About halfway through the movie, I quit expecting to see flashes of Jennifer naked and tied in a dungeon—the family seems normal and wholesome.

It's amazing to see how Voxx became the smart, capable male he is today. He was shaped that way by a cool mom and caring dad.

"Hello, son." Verris makes his first appearance on the screen. He could be Voxx's older brother; they look so much alike. I guess it makes sense if human DNA just gets obliterated by stronger Zinn genes. "Hello, nameless, faceless female. Sorry, that's what Jennifer has been calling you for over three decades, it's hard not to call you that.

"But we know your name now, Victoria. I've been around Jennifer long enough to know what you must think of Voxx and me. You probably think this practice is barbaric and inhumane. Maybe it is. My son abducted you, after all.

"I hope you can learn to love Voxx even half as much as my beloved Jennifer loves me. I also hope you choose to meet Jennifer and me in person on Choosing Day. We will welcome you into our family and love you like our own daughter."

The vid flicks off. I'm left gazing out the windows into the vast expanse of space. Voxx pulls me closer and arranges my head on his pec.

"Now I know what you meant by 'puff piece'," his voice rumbles in his chest. Even though he just cracked his first official joke, I can tell he's choking back a lot of emotion.

"You were an awesome kid. I didn't expect to see the compassion you showed to your physically handicapped neighbor or your uncle and aunt who couldn't conceive. You were wise as a child."

He kisses my head. "It's amazing to see myself through the eyes of someone who loves me so much. I never doubted her love, but seeing this was… special. Tell me about your childhood… if you want."

"There's not much to tell."

"If you don't want to talk about it, that's okay."

"What do you want to know?" My childhood was so ordinary.

"Everything. What made you so smart and funny and strong?"

"Funny? You think I'm funny? You have no sense of humor."

"I do too have a sense of humor. Yours just had to grow on me."

"Well, you have things that are growing on me, too." Crap, I shouldn't have admitted that.

"Like what?" He waggles his eyebrows suggestively.

"Your cooking," I say with a straight face.

"Tell me about growing up in Iowa. I want to understand you better."

I pause. How do you explain your whole childhood to someone who grew up on Zinn?

"We have lots more time together, zara. Tell me one story tonight that will help me understand who you are."

Why this one? Why does this story come hurtling at me from the past? I don't know, but this is the story my brain wants me to share.

"Fifth grade, that would make me about ten years old. Mom tried her hand at sewing. Even at that age I protested wearing it. The dress just wasn't... cool. But I didn't want to hurt her feelings, so I wore the Little-House-on-the-Prairie dress.

"Jimmy Cranston—God, I remember his name and everything about that day like it was yesterday—Jimmy Cranston started teasing me on the bus. When we got to school, the merciless insults spread and soon almost everyone in my class was relentless about that old-fashioned blue dress.

"It was awful for a ten-year-old." I shrug, still not understanding why this is the story I chose to share instead of telling him how I was chosen to speak at my high school graduation or how well I did in mock trials in law school.

He's quiet for a moment.

"Bedtime?" I ask, ready to move on.

"Why that story, Victoria? Why did you pick that to share?"

"Not sure."

"It shaped you. It made you want to conform. Be normal. Fit in."

"I guess so."

"You wore that dress because you didn't want to say no to your mother. And that day you learned you didn't like to be different. Is that why the idea of liking what we share in the bedroom bothers you? Why you fight it so much? Because it's not the status quo?"

Is it? That day did shape me. Even Avery, my best girlfriend from high school, accused me of being 'vanilla' when she showed me the collar she wore.

It's late. I can't think. "Bedtime?" I ask. I don't even want to have my ten minutes tonight. As Scarlett O'Hara would say, 'Tomorrow is another day'.

Day Five

Voxx

Yesterday is over, Voxx has disappeared, and Sir is back—with a vengeance. I've been re-reading the manuals and recalling my father's advice—I've got to maintain strict control. The first thing I must do is re-establish my dominance.

"Wake up, Victoria. I want you in the kitchen making me breakfast in five minutes." I put on my clothes and tie back my hair. My moments of weakness yesterday, along with letting her see that vid, have destroyed the dominant relationship I've been building. She needs to remember I'm in charge.

Three minutes later, she's in the kitchen, her long, brown hair knotted around itself to keep it out of her eyes.

"Cook me *chernoy* for breakfast like I taught you yesterday." I saunter to the captain's chair and work on star charts. Every time I glance at her, she looks perplexed and worried. The sounds and smells emanating from the kitchen don't inspire confidence.

"Sir."

"Yes."

"Your breakfast is ready," her voice is nervous, tight.

"Serve it to me," I tell her when I'm seated at the bar.

"I… uh."

She dumps it on a plate and sets it in front of me along with utensils and a napkin. After taking one bite, I glance up to find her biting her lip, her brows lowered.

"Taste." I beckon her closer and put a forkful in her mouth. "Barrister, what's your verdict?"

"It's not as good as yours, Sir."

"Correct. You will apologize and then tell me the correct ingredients and the proper steps. I'll confirm you've got it correct, and you can begin again after you put this in the garbage."

"I'm sorry, Sir." She looks contrite. Perhaps this is how people apologize on Earth.

"On Zinn, when a female displeases her male, there is an expected ritual."

"What is that, Sir?"

She's going to hate this. Hate is perhaps not a strong enough word. "Kneel." I point to the floor in front of me. When she's in position, my feet are on the bottom rung about a foot below her face.

"Eyes down. Touch the sides of my feet with your hands and put your forehead on my instep. When you apologize, you say what you did wrong, how you will correct your behavior in the future, and say you're sorry in the most sincere way. A good mate takes this as an opportunity to express her deepest affection for her male."

I watch a panoply of emotions cross her face and can quantify each one: shock, anger, humiliation, and acceptance. On the issue of how to present a proper apology, I didn't expect acceptance from Victoria—ever.

She takes a deep breath, cradles my feet in her hands and sets her head down. She's working up her nerve to follow my directions. I wonder if she's walked back from acceptance and is securely in hatred territory about now.

"Sir, I wasn't mindful enough yesterday when you were teaching me. I assumed you'd always be here to help me. This morning I winged it without heeding the consequences or asking for help. Maybe I feared disappointing you, but that is no excuse.

"If you'll talk me through it, I'll pay better attention and when I cook this dish for you I'll endeavor to perfectly follow every direction. I'm very sorry I didn't perform better. I apologize for disappointing you, Sir."

Her entire speech was spoken to the tops of my feet. I still can't see her facial expressions. What's the word I learned on Facebook? Is she punking me and pretending sincerity meanwhile rolling her eyes at me? I prefer to accept her apology at face value. I'll have plenty of time to watch her later.

If I was a stronger Zinn, I would allow her to worry about her offensive behavior and possible punishment for hours. But I'm weak. I can't wait to finish breakfast and dash to the bedroom with her.

Tilting her chin to me, I spear her with a penetrating gaze, still wondering if she's playing me. She's not avoiding my eyes, though, so I'll give her the benefit of the doubt.

"Apology accepted." She recites the steps and ingredients, and I watch her cook the *chernoy* again. This effort is edible, and I let it go at that. There will be plenty of time to refine her cooking technique in the future—if we have a future.

"Do you remember what's on our agenda for today?" I ask after she's cleaned the galley.

"I'm to 'learn you', Sir."

"And do you have any idea what that means?"

"I assume I'll learn how to pleasure you, Sir."

"That and much more. Please take a shower. I've left out several perfumes for you to choose from. When you're ready, kneel at the foot of the bed and call me. Might I remind you I forbid you to use my given name."

"Yes, Sir."

She calls me fifteen minutes later. When I enter the bedroom, she's kneeling at the foot of the bed, facing the doorway.

"Perfect position, Victoria. Good girl. While I shower I want you to reflect on the care I have given your body over these past few days. Do you have any doubt that your pleasure has always been in the forefront of my thoughts?"

"No, Sir. You've always strived to provide for my pleasure, often at the expense of your own."

"I'd like you to quiet your mind and give thought to the lengths you will go to extend the same generosity to me."

Victoria

The past four days have been an education for me in many ways. It's still the middle of the morning and I've already gone through a whirlwind of emotions.

At first, I was petulant and didn't want to have to make breakfast for him, especially after his curt order to cook for him. Then I felt embarrassed for presenting him inedible *chernoy*. He's a harsh man, but he's provided me with many creature comforts that weren't mandated in the Interstellar Compact.

His culture is far different from mine and he's a dominant alpha male for sure, but he never fed me crappy food or provided inferior clothes—when he gave me clothes—or gave the slightest indication he didn't care about my comforts or desires.

I was truly repentant for not taking care with his breakfast.

As much as I enjoyed Voxx last night, as much as it was a relief not having to pose in uncomfortable positions, I have to admit I like submitting to him at times like these.

This male has brought me to the heights of pleasure countless times. He masturbates in the bathroom, but he's never forced himself on me. I'm willing to 'learn him', in fact, I'm eager.

Clearing my mind, I promise myself I will be as diligent about his pleasure today as he's been about mine.

He stalks out of the bathroom amid a haze of steam. He's naked and beautiful. His muscles bunch under his skin as he sinks to his knees across from me on the floor at the foot of the bed.

"We're moving into uncharted territory for you, Victoria. There are certain… rules that are inviolate. We need to review them now."

"Yes, Sir."

He grabs my hands in his and waits for my gaze to meet his.

"You're a generous person. You grew up on Earth. I imagine it will seem like second nature for you to want to initiate activities with me today. I appreciate any desire you have to show me your ingenuity or initiative or even some affection. I forbid you taking any liberties today that I haven't specified.

"Today you must be very mindful of taking my direction and only my direction. Is that clear?"

"Yes, Sir. I will do only as you say."

"Music to my ears, *zara*."

He sits on the edge of the bed and tells me to stand behind him and brush his hair.

"Until we leave this room, Victoria, it will be much easier for you if you cease labeling me as your captor, your enemy, or the purple asshole. You will find it much more tolerable if you find your inner submissive and put your energies into pleasing me. I'd like you to brush my hair with the same attention to detail and enjoyment that I provided for you when I brushed yours."

He's right. It will be easier for me, and for him. Ordering my thoughts into a Zen holding pattern, I focus only on brushing his hair. I notice every aspect of the silky strands, the shimmering white coloring, the pattern of his hairline. I brush from his forehead to his neck, then tilt his head forward so I can brush upward from his nape to the top of his head.

I pay close attention to how relaxed his shoulder muscles become. I find the right rhythm and just the right pressure to calm him. Soon his breathing is slower and when I lean to the side, I see his lashes have drifted down onto his cheeks.

It's a pleasure, really, to provide him pleasure. I don't think I ever learned that with my previous lovers. I hope I can remember this for my future boyfriends when I get back to Earth. I could do this all day, but I know I won't get the chance. Pretty soon his mammoth cock will be jammed in my mouth or some other orifice. I better get Zen with that right away.

"Good girl, Victoria. There's oil on the bedside table. I'd like you to straddle my waist and learn how to pleasure my back. I'll make appreciative noises when you hit the right spots so it will be easy to figure me out. Because, as you'll remember, you were kind enough to make appreciative noises to help me find some of your very pleasurable spots."

I blush, but he's already face down on the mattress, his arms bent at the elbows, hands above his head.

"Sir," I ask, "can you ask the *Drayant* to play the perfect calming music?"

He does. The relaxing music surrounding us resembles that of fancy spas on Earth. I straddle him and suck in a shocked breath. My open core on his warm, purple skin is arousing. As I lean down to whisper in his ear, my pebbled nipples trace two lines on his back.

"Sir," my voice is a hushed whisper, "I'm going to get you wet. I already am."

"It gives me great joy to have that effect on you, little Victoria. Please continue."

My hands seek the outlines of the long, strong muscles I see beneath his lovely skin. My fingers learn when to skim the surface and when to dig in deep, when to rub and when to knead.

At first, he praised with words, then with soft animal noises that were as eloquent as a poem, and by the end of the massage I needed no more tutelage.

When my hands dipped below his waist, he said, "No," and I didn't attempt it again. After my first hour on his ship, he let me put up boundaries. I'm giving him the same control.

He flips over and pulls the bedcovers up to his waist. "Straddle me and learn my chest." A brief smile slashes across his face then disappears.

His eyes are closed, and he's already relaxed. He's given me free rein. My fingers dig into the tight muscles of his neck and shoulders, reaching around and under him to get to the spots that make him moan.

Touching him is a lesson in anatomy. I don't know all their names, but I can feel every muscle. I've never been with a guy who had a six-pack. Tracing the outline of each tight rectangle, I find what brings him pleasure.

I make a conscious decision to disobey when I lean forward and slide my fingers up the corded steel of his neck to touch his face. He doesn't stop me, so I'm emboldened. I memorize the hard line of his chin and the straight bone of his nose. I trace the arc of each eyebrow, then ruffle his eyelashes with one finger—this makes him smile.

I hadn't paid attention before, but now I'm fascinated by the contrast of our skin—my pink against his purple. It's sexy, alluring.

Speaking of sexy, even though we're separated by one sheet and a thin blanket, his cock pulses against my core. It's especially noticeable when I lean up to touch his scalp. This male has steely control. He has to know I'd flip this little exercise from innocent to full-blown raging animal in a heartbeat if he gave the word. But no words are given.

"Very good, Victoria. I'll make you lunch." He grasps my wrists and brings each hand to his lips where he kisses the pad of each finger, one at a time. My clit flutters at the sensual sweetness of this act. "Thank you," he says as he rolls out from under me and slides off the bed.

I stand and watch that magnificent backside saunter into the bathroom. The two divots a few inches above the crack in his ass are the sexiest things in the galaxy.

I imagine he's stroking that thick, purple cock right now. He's been erect and throbbing since we started this little exercise in frustration. So have I. Well, not the erect part, but the throbbing part. I've had orgasms since we met, lots of them. Most of them were earth-shattering. He, however, has only found release in the palm of his hand. Which is a surprise, especially today. I thought for certain he was going to let down his self-erected barriers and have sex with me just now.

I'm still watching the shiny metal door, waiting for his return, as I ponder things. If he comes out, throws me on the bed and demands sex, how will I respond? I know he can do anything he wants to me. He's stronger than me and more forceful. He could tie me up and fuck me to his heart's content. Which evokes a strong, pulsing clench in my core.

I guess I just answered my own question. If he were to want sex, I'd be happy to oblige. Jennifer told me I should go with the flow. I'd already come to that conclusion myself. I might as well quit fighting.

I jump down the rabbit hole with both feet when I wonder why he isn't pouncing on me, throwing me onto the mattress, and having his way with me. Luckily my crazy thoughts are interrupted when he emerges from the bathroom. He's taken a quick shower. I hadn't even noticed how much time has passed.

"What are you doing?" He looks mystified.

"Standing here, Sir."

"Why?"

Why *am* I standing here? I glance at the clock and see it's been fifteen minutes or more and I've just been motionless, waiting for him to come out.

"I have no idea."

"I do." He grabs my hand and pulls me into the kitchen where he sets me on the counter.

"Care to share, Sir?"

"You were waiting for direction."

"What do you mean?"

"You were waiting for me to tell you what to do." He's already pulled some food off the shelf, but he stalks back over and holds my chin between his fingers so I can't look away when he says, "Like a true submissive."

My eyes flare open, then slam shut. Fuck. Fuckity fuck. Is that true? Of course it is. Heresy. Blasphemy. No, it can't be! I'd be a traitor to my sex if that was true. But, a little voice in my head tells me, it is.

"That's ridiculous," I protest weakly.

"I'm standing right here. Your face is an open book. You know I'm right, but I won't argue." He turns around and starts cooking.

"Sir, can I borrow your computer pad to use the Zinn version of the Internet?"

"Sure, wait a moment." He stirs the contents of a pot, then retrieves a pad that looks a lot like what we have on Earth. "This is for your use. Keep it. Everything's in English, and I rigged it to keep you out of any sites the government has deemed off-limits."

I don't protest that it shouldn't matter since my mind will be wiped, anyway. Besides, what I'll be looking up has nothing to do with state secrets. I search 'female submission'.

He's going to serve lunch far too soon for me to do a deep dive into the subject, but upon quick perusal, I think he's right. I even had time to answer an online test, swiped, I assume, right off Earth's Internet. It says I'm 74% submissive. That's not too bad, is it? I groan.

"Lunch. *Eboi Plantay*, one of my specialties."

He sets a plate in front of me; it looks divine and smells delicious. As opposed to my attempt at breakfast, he's taken great care to cook and present this dish. Without thinking, I wait for him to take his first bite before I taste mine.

I'm a submissive. It hits me with the speed and force of a freight train.

I do things like this all the time; I always have. My mind runs through a hundred pictures demonstrating proof that I was a total submissive in every relationship back on Earth. I always let my girlfriends decide where to go for lunch. I seldom had a strong preference for what movie we'd see. I deferred to every friend, boyfriend, my parents, and even my siblings. I wore the stupid blue dress in fifth grade to please my mom FFS.

"You aren't hungry? You haven't taken a bite. Did *Eboi Plantay* get bad Yelp reviews back on Earth?" He cocks his head. His second attempt at a joke in as many days.

He leans close and feeds me a forkful.

"Mmmm," I say before I even chew. "Delish," I pronounce after my first bite. Actually, I don't know what it tastes like because it's like sawdust in my mouth. I'm not hungry. I can't taste. I'm gobsmacked by the realization that I'm a submissive and I'd never given it any thought before.

"Not hungry?"

"Nope." Whoops. "Sir."

"Open your legs."

I follow his directions immediately.

"Good girl," he says as he slips a finger inside my folds and slides from top to bottom. He holds up his finger for me to inspect, but I'm not certain what he wants me to see.

"Dry," he informs me when it's obvious I don't know what he wants.

Oh.

"Go to the red square."

"Yes, Sir."

I hurry over and stand, eyes on him, waiting for my next command.

"New position—Bend. Legs wide hands on knees, bend over. It's also called Punishment position."

"Yes, Sir."

I comply, with alacrity.

"Point that beautiful ass toward me, Victoria."

"Yes, Sir."

Oh my God. Why am I in the Punishment Position?

"Remember you can say the word 'red' if there's something you don't want to do."

"Yes, Sir."

I didn't realize not eating his lunch would earn me a punishment or I would have shoveled it in my cakehole,

"Sir, I'm sorry for anything I did to offend you."

"The only words allowed out of your mouth until further notice are 'yes, Sir' and 'thank you'. Unless you say 'red'. Do you understand?"

"Yes, Sir."

"Put your hands on your calves. I want to see every pink fold."

"Yes, Sir."

"Ass higher in the air," he barks.

"Yes, Sir."

"Hands even lower, on your ankles. Head up, thrust your breasts out."

He walks to the wall of torture, grabs a different whip, a quirt I believe it's called. Its handle is shorter than the riding crop and it has three leather thongs on the abuse end.

"I'm sorry, Sir, for whatever I did."

He uses the handle to lift my chin an inch, then slides the shaft through my folds.

"Freeze."

I stop immediately, wondering if I'm supposed to say, 'yes, Sir' or not when I'm frozen. I opt for observing the freeze command.

"Lift your ass even higher and open your legs more so I can have access to your most intimate parts."

I fucking hate you. "Yes, Sir."

I position myself to his specifications and wait.

He steps even closer and glides his hand down my back, over the swell of my bottom and dips into my sex. My hips thrust to help his fingers penetrate, but there is no penetration.

When he places his fingers and part of his palm in front of my face, I see they're glistening with my wetness from just that quick swipe through my folds.

"You're wet."

"Yes, Sir."

"Lick it off me."

"Yes, Sir."

"Every drop."

"Yes, Sir."

"Good girl. Close your eyes and pay complete attention to your pelvis, your clit, your core. Tell me what you feel. Leave nothing out."

"I'm horny, Sir. I'm dripping wet. My channel is clenching. I feel… need. My clit… my clit is pulsing."

He inches closer, slides my feet farther apart with his foot and shoves two fingers inside me.

"Describe that."

"Heaven, Sir. It's so good to have you inside me." I clench him tightly with my inner muscles. He presses the heel of his hand against my clit and circles it. I gasp—intense pleasure.

"Would you like release?"

"Oh, yes, Sir."

"Beg me."

I don't hesitate even a moment. "Please, Sir, may I come?"

"More begging."

"Please, Sir, I would love to come. I would do anything for you if you'd let me come."

"Would you suck my cock?"

"Yes, Sir."

"Say it."

"Please, Sir, if you let me come I'll suck your magnificent purple cock, you have but to ask."

He adds another finger inside me and circles his thumb on my clit and in less than a minute I spasm into ecstasy. Deep, hard muscle contractions spiral through me. Not just in my pelvis but throughout my body. Long, loud moans escape my throat, and I reach out, happy to touch the arm that just provided so much pleasure.

"Thank you, Sir. Thank you."

He pets me and pulls me up so my head rests against his peck as I return slowly to this world. He pulled his fingers out of me which makes me feel empty. I didn't want him to leave. I liked the feel of him inside me. His other arm is stroking my back, quietly caressing me.

I float back into reality and realize I'm swimming in confusion. What just happened? Did I really just beg for release after punishment? Was there even a reason he punished me? How fucked up am I?

His fingers circle my wrist and he pulls me to kneel next to the captain's chair.

"Tell me what just happened." His tone is hard.

I'm having trouble looking him in the eye. "You tell me, Sir."

He scolds me with his glance. "Start at the part where I said your folds were dry."

I'm not certain what he wants to hear. As I play it over in my head, I realize everything. Air seeps through my lips in a long huff. "Oh, my God. I'm a true submissive." My eyes plead with him to disagree, but he simply nods his head.

"Tell me what happened," he prods.

"You objectified me and ordered me around and made me think you were going to physically punish me and every single thing you did turned me on. I'm a freak."

The word self-loathing doesn't begin to cover what I'm experiencing right now.

"You're not a freak. You're a submissive." He waits for me to digest his pronouncement.

"It's not normal for a woman's pussy to get drenched when she's treated like a possession for your enjoyment. I imagine there's a diagnosis for that," I say.

"It's normal for *you*, Victoria."

"You knew before I did," it's an accusatory whisper.

"Yes. I was looking for clues. You were desperately trying to ignore them."

"I know this is against the rules, Sir, but can I have two hours alone? To think?"

He considers for a moment, then nods. "Be kneeling at my feet in one-hundred-twenty minutes. And Victoria?"

"Yes, Sir."

"No matter what discussion you have in the privacy of your mind. No matter what conclusions you come to in the next two hours, I want you in perfect Kneeling form in one-hundred-twenty minutes saying only the words 'yes, Sir', 'thank you', and 'please make me come' unless you're given permission to speak your mind."

"Yes, Sir."

I grab the pad and scurry to the bedroom mentally thanking him for that last remark. It gives me something to hang onto—my hatred—other than all the questions swirling in my head.

Jumping back onto the Internet, I search kink sites. I realize this stuff wasn't stolen from Earth's Internet, it *is* Earth's Internet. I was going to ask questions about my newly discovered fetish, but maybe I can contact someone to rescue me.

My elation at possible escape plummets quickly. What exactly would I say? 'I've been abducted by a big purple guy who's holding me captive and forcing me to orgasm every ten minutes'? Or how about starting it with, 'I'm somewhere in space…'? Or maybe, 'our evil government is selling our bodies in exchange for military-grade weapons'?

Yeah, I'll be about as believable as Voxx was when I woke up on his sex table. I labeled him 'looney tunes' and, oh, yeah, 'batshit crazy'.

Even if someone believed me, I have no idea where I am. And the big purple asshole in the next room is probably monitoring my correspondence, anyway.

I remind myself of my original goal—to get feedback from another living sentient being about the crazy shit that's floating through my head.

I jump into a kink community chatroom, register as 'GoodGirl' and type.

GoodGirl: *What's wrong with me?*

Spank Me Daddy: *What's going on?*

GoodGirl: *I'm in a new relationship with a guy who treats me like shit. Well, no, he tries to be nice, but he orders me around.*

Spank Me Daddy: *He's your Dom?*

GoodGirl: *He's super dominant but I'm not a submissive. Well, that's not true. I didn't know I was a submissive until about an hour ago when I realized my body responds like Pavlov's dog to his commands.*

Spank Me Daddy: *So, he's dominant and you're submissive and it turns you on? Where's the problem?*

GoodGirl: *I don't want to be a submissive.*

Spank Me Daddy: *In the words of Frank Zappa, 'You Are What You Is'.*

GoodGirl: *Okay, so maybe I am a submissive. I don't want to be submissive to him.*

Spank Me Daddy: *Some doms are mean, some don't understand your needs, if that's the case, you need to get out of the relationship and run like hell. There are all kinds in the kink community. You don't have to stay with one of the bad ones.*

GoodGirl: *Define bad.*

Spank Me Daddy: *They hurt you in ways you don't like. They don't see to your needs. They don't provide aftercare. They don't respect your safe word. You do have a safe word, don't you?*

GoodGirl: *Yes.*

Spank Me Daddy: *Does he respect you when you use it?*

GoodGirl: *I've never used it.*

Spank Me Daddy: *Why? Would he punish you if you use it?*

GoodGirl: *No. He keeps reminding me to use it if I want.*

Spank Me Daddy: *Okay. He sounds pretty legit. What about aftercare? After a scene does he hold you? Keep you warm? Talk if you want or stay quiet if you want? Make sure you're hydrated?*

GoodGirl: *Well, yeah.*

Spank Me Daddy: *Does he attend to your sexual needs? Does he turn you on? Are you attracted to him? No matter how 'kinky', does his touch please you?*

He's probably reading every word I'm writing in real-time. My face heats as I reply.

GoodGirl: *Yes.*

Spank Me Daddy: *Yes to all that? He sounds like a great dom.*

GoodGirl: *Well, he's not. Maybe it's because things were out of hand when we met. He broke a lot of boundaries at first and we got off to a very bad start.*

Spank Me Daddy: *Communication is key, goodgirl. Have you talked about this? Has he apologized? Has he never made the same mistakes again? The D/s lifestyle is difficult to traverse. Is he new to it, too?*

GoodGirl: *Yes. I'm his first.*

Spank Me Daddy: *That explains a lot. You have to give some benefit of the doubt. There's a lot for subs to learn, but also a lot for Doms—actually more.*

GoodGirl: *I know it's not politically correct, but we're from vastly different cultures. Maybe that's the problem.*

Spank Me Daddy: *I don't want to sound judgmental, but don't you think you're grasping at straws? I mean, how different is he? He's from Earth, right? LOL*

Out of all the things she could have said, why would she say that? Am I actually having a conversation with Voxx? I pad to the door and peek out. He's puttering in the kitchen—nope, not him.

GoodGirl: *Sometimes you wouldn't think so. LOL*

Spank Me Daddy: *I'm no shrink, but it sounds like the problem's with you. Maybe you're not ready for the lifestyle.*

Well, yeah, that's why I'm asking for help. But Spank Me's trying hard to be helpful. It's not her fault that my situation is a little… out there.

GoodGirl: *Maybe you're right. You've been helpful. I'll give things more thought. TTYL*

Spank Me Daddy: *TTYL*

I glance at the clock and see I have seven minutes left, so I splash water on my face and take a deep breath, mentally preparing myself to face him.

Two hours of soul-searching, one conversation with Spank Me Daddy, and searing self-honesty and I've come to several conclusions.

One, I'm a submissive. I've always been one. When I think back on my childhood, I realize it started when I was young. It's hard-wired.

Two, I still hate him. That's not going to change.

Three, I'm totally freaking attracted to him. His touch lights me on fire. That's not going to change, either.

Four, we're on this ship for nine more days. I need to do whatever it takes to keep my sanity.

Five, I'm going to give in to my every desire for the next nine days. I have to follow his rules anyway, and he gives me mind-bending pleasure. Besides, it's not like I'll remember any of this when I get back to my regular life, anyway. It will all be wiped away. Sanitized. I won't even remember I'm a submissive when I get back home. If I kept it a secret from myself for twenty-six years, I can keep it a secret for the rest of my life.

Case closed. I'll enjoy the sex. I'll walk on the wild side and give in to my kinky desires and go home. And because Voxx is such a prick, I won't even feel guilty about leaving him womanless for the rest of his fucking life.

There. Problem solved.

Voxx

She's kneeling at my feet in one-hundred-nineteen minutes. Her position is perfect. Her pink nipples are pebbled. Her eyes are red from crying.

I've always known I was dominant. It was never a shock or an epiphany. Of course, every male on my planet is built this way—it was expected. It's hard to relate to Victoria's reaction to finding this new revelation that she's a submissive.

I hadn't anticipated how difficult it would be for her to accept this aspect of herself. It's considered a fetish on her planet. She repulses herself. She'll need help getting over this hurdle. I should abandon my plans for tonight.

"Want to talk?" I ask, my tone neutral.

"No, Sir," her words are clipped.

She's closed herself off. Although I don't like it, I'll give her more time.

"What's your favorite Earth movie?"

"*Avatar*."

"Come sit on my lap and watch it with me."

She looks at me accusingly, as if suggesting we watch her favorite movie is a punishment—or a trick.

"Wait. I'll be right back."

I grab some pants from our room and slip them on, then return. She'll be more comfortable if I'm clothed.

I dip into an Earth database and project the movie on the windows at the front of the bridge, then pat my lap. She climbs up and gets comfortable.

"Science Fiction. I've watched several of your Earth science fiction movies. They're usually quite humorous."

"Yes, Sir," she snips, letting me know she doesn't appreciate my sarcasm.

"You have to admit, Robby the Robot was hilarious."

"It was before my time, Sir. Oh…" She looks down in exaggerated deference, "Can I speak words other than 'yes and Sir'?"

"Yes. You may say 'thank you, Sir', and 'please make me come'." I feel every muscle in her body stiffen so I tip her face to mine. "Joking."

"It's difficult to be with someone with no sense of humor who tries to joke." She tosses her head.

I pull her next to me, settle her head on my pec, and kiss the top of her head. She'll come around.

"That movie was entertaining," I tell her when the credits roll. "Very good. Much better than Robby the Robot."

"Yes, Sir," she still sounds distant and disinterested.

"Interesting that your favorite movie is about blue aliens."

"Yes, Sir. Nice blue aliens who want to be partners with their females. As opposed to mean, overbearing, controlling purple aliens who want to dominate and command. Worlds apart."

"My favorite part of the movie is when the female says, 'I see you'. I see you, Victoria. I know who you are. I see your beautiful form and I'm trying to understand the thoughts and emotions inside your head."

She doesn't respond.

"The next nine days will be interminable if we don't talk, Victoria. Shall we call a truce?"

"If you say so, Sir," she's just saying what I want to hear.

"Yes. I say so."

A true dominant should never do what I'm about to do, but I've been considering it through most of the movie and I'm going to do it, anyway. Victoria is a special female and I've already learned that using common Zinn practices won't convince her to make the right decision on Choosing Day. I need to trust my own instincts.

"Are you hungry or do you want to skip dinner?" I might as well get the disturbing conversation out of the way. I assume the mere topic of food is going to set off a firestorm.

"Am I to be punished if I don't love everything you cook for me, *Sir*?"

"Your tone is bordering on sassy, Victoria. Repeat yourself without the defiance." I wait, hating that she's making this harder for both of us to put this in the past.

"Never mind. I know that wasn't why I was punished," her tone is repentant.

"Good. You're correct. It wasn't actually punishment, was it? It was to prove a point."

"Yes, Sir."

"I had an activity planned for tonight in bed, but I want to give you a choice. We can go to sleep early and start fresh tomorrow. What did you call it, an overdo?"

"A do-over, Sir."

"So, activities in bed, or sleeping in bed?" Every single one of my countrymen would shake their heads in rebuke if they heard my question. But I feel good about it. It's best for Victoria, and that's what matters.

She tucks her head under my chin and is quiet for so long I wonder if she's being disobedient. When I tip her chin to look at me, though, she's biting her bottom lip and deep in thought. At this point, I wonder if I should decide for her, but that would defeat the purpose.

"Tell me what you're debating."

Her eyes fly open then crash shut. I hear her molars clamp shut. "Tell me now," I insist.

"Sir, please, can I have one thing to call my own? My thoughts?"

She leans closer so her lips are at my ear and I can't inspect her face. "You can put things in my body without my permission. You can touch me whenever and however you want. You can order me around into impossible postures. I have so little control over anything. Anything. Please, can I keep my thoughts to myself?"

"For this process to work, Victoria, you should tell me. I want to hear what you're struggling with, but I won't order it."

She throws her arms around my neck and ducks back under my chin.

"Give me a moment." She pauses for several minutes, but her hands cling to me like I'm her lifeline. I'll wait. "I want to do what you want," she says. She's still hiding from me, avoiding all eye contact.

"Tell me why," my voice is firm. I'm all but ordering her. I want her to find her place in our relationship, and the way for her to do that is by asking herself these tough questions.

"I—"

Pulling her away from me, I set her on my knees so she can't hide anymore.

"I—"

She's looking at my chest.

"Look at me, Victoria."

She takes a deep breath and answers in a nervous rush. "I'm embarrassed and don't want to admit the things my body wants. I'd rather be transported back to my bed on Earth right now and not have to deal with any of these… aberrant desires.

"But I'm here and I decided I'm going to allow things to play out. So if you want to romp in bed tonight, count me in."

I gather her in my arms and hold her tight. "Good girl, little Victoria. You're smart and strong and you know the word 'red' will stop things. You do know that, right? Today with the Bend posture? I would have stopped immediately. Even the punishments, Victoria. Are you aware that I'll stop even those if you but ask? Tell me you understand."

"If I say 'red', you'll stop whatever you're doing. I can say 'red' at any time, Sir."

"Good girl."

I kiss the top of her head, but that's not good enough. I want to reconnect with her, she's been in her head too long and that always sets her back. Cradling her head with my hand, I hold her in place and crush my lips to hers.

I suck her bottom lip into my mouth and nip it. My tongue tears through her defenses and ransacks her mouth. I touch everywhere, claiming every inch. "Mine," I growl.

This, what we're doing right now is the embodiment of what's playing out between us on every level. I take, she allows. I claim, she yields. But she has to understand that she's a willing party to her own surrender. I kiss her over and over. Hard, plundering kisses. She's panting and is so soft, so pliant in my embrace.

I stop and stay still as a statue as I contemplate my next offer. I want her to understand that in a way, the submissive has almost total power in a relationship. "You have ten minutes right now, little Victoria. You tell me exactly what you want. I'll comply."

She looks fearful, like Argyle when she peed on the floor before we properly trained her, afraid we'd punish her.

"Anything goes, little Victoria. Anything." My gaze is hard on her, like I'm looking into her soul.

She puts my hands on her breasts. I leave them where she put them. Closing her eyes, she breathes deep to gather strength. "Pluck my nipples, Sir. Until I beg. Then make me come."

Victoria

That kiss, that one stupid kiss liquified my skin. I'm on fire for him from just a kiss. Straddling him with my knees on either side of his hips in his captain's chair, I grind on him, painting his black pants with my honey. His fingers pluck and coax one nipple into a hard bud of yearning, even as he bends to suckle the other one into his mouth.

I'm pressing myself against him so hard I'm close to release already. I grab his hand to pull it to my groin, I want to force his fingers into me. No, I want so much more than that, but I'll settle for that right this minute.

"No, tell me what you want. Don't show, don't ask—tell me.

"Fuck me, Sir. Put your fingers in me."

I'm desperate. This frenzied need barreled up on me out of nowhere. I scramble up, my feet on the seat so I have more freedom of movement. I'm not waiting for his fingers to fuck me, I'm fucking his fingers.

A low, keening moan escapes my mouth. No, it's not escaping, it's been streaming out of me for long minutes. I'm an animal. I'm out of control. I bite his neck. Not a nip, but a full-on, toothful bite that probably drew blood.

An orgasm rips through me, tearing me apart from the inside and rearranging me down to a molecular level. It almost stops and then kicks in again as wave after wave of bliss brings me to physical paradise over and over.

My muscles are screaming in the agony and ecstasy of physical release. My face is a tight rictus of pain and pleasure, and my throat's on fire from moaning during this non-stop rollercoaster of an orgasm. I settle back into the real world abruptly, remembering I'm in Voxx's arms, on a spaceship for some reason I don't remember.

I still hate him, and he's kissing me and petting the top of my head. And even in the crazy shape I'm in, I realize I should probably go down on him to give him some relief. He has to be ready to explode after being in my arms, witnessing my physical rapture.

My clumsy post-orgasmic fingers fumble at his waistband, but he firmly says, "No," then goes back to petting me.

"Feel good?" he asks, genuinely interested.

"Mmm-hmm." My lips are too numb to talk.

"You want this?" He uses my hand to stroke himself over his zipper.

"Yes. Sir."

"I think you need dinner. Then you'll learn me."

"I'd like that, Sir."

After what we just shared in his captain's chair, I think any residual embarrassment should be long gone.

~.~

What have I had, like a hundred orgasms already today? Yet I'm dripping wet before I hit the bedroom. And how crazy is it that I'm so excited about 'learning him'? I should hate him. I *do* hate him. But I want to provide him pleasure. I've lost my mind, that's no secret.

Shut up, Tori. You already decided you were going to dive into this experience wholeheartedly. Do it, I tell myself.

He pulls me into the bedroom and stands us both at the foot of the bed.

"You have permission to learn me, Victoria. You may touch me any way you like. I won't be shy about letting you know my reactions. My cock cannot enter your body—that's the only rule. Until tomorrow.

"Undress me nice and slow. As if I'm a present you've been waiting to unwrap for a long time."

He usually waltzes around nude all day, sometimes he wears those ubiquitous black cargo pants, but he's added a thin black sweater to the mix. I guess I get to unwrap more of the package.

Slipping my hands under his sweater, I slide my fingers up his sides to his underarms, then down. I edge toward his six-pack, memorizing the ridges and hollows of his warm skin. I was nervous a moment ago, but now I'm warming to the task as I realize he's just standing here, giving me free rein.

My thumbs find his little nipples and circle there for a moment. He's trying not to show any reaction, but his nostrils flare. Oh, goody. I pluck the tiny nubs with two fingers and I spy the slightest pinch of his lips. Somebody likes their nipples played with.

I slide my hands up around his shoulders and delight in every muscled curve. Then I come back to his masculine nipples and pluck again—this time harder. This earns me the slightest hip thrust. I've found a magic weapon.

Stepping behind him, I splay my hands open across the expanse of his muscled back and glide from shoulders to waist and back again. He's such a big guy, without an ounce of fat. I love exploring the hard ridges beneath his skin.

Lifting his top up without taking it off, I want to drag my nipples across his flesh, but I'm too short, or should I say he's too tall? I spy a little stool in the corner and the thought strikes me that there's no reason for it to be on this ship other than for what I'm about to do.

I carry it over, set it behind him and step onto it. Now I lift the back of his sweater and slide my hardened peaks along his warm flesh. He grunts softly.

Pressing myself against him even more tightly, I reach around him and pull his nipples. As he thrusts back against me, my thoughts toggle from noticing the sensual feelings I'm kindling in him, to my own responses. I'm already beyond aroused. My core is dripping, my nipples ache, and the only thought pulsing in my head is need.

My tongue flicks my teeth, reminding me of what I want to be doing to certain parts of his anatomy.

I tug his top over his head, toss it on the floor, then lean back to drink in the sight of him. I've seen him naked just about all day every day, but somehow it feels different now. His body is male perfection—purple skin and all.

"Your body is beautiful, Sir."

He says nothing, just reaches around, grabs one of my ass cheeks and snugs my hips against him.

I comb my fingers through his long white hair. It's a stark contrast against his purple skin. He presses his head against my palm, evidently enjoying having his head petted as much as I do.

Up on my high perch, I reach over his shoulders and enjoy every inch of his muscled chest. Peeking down the broad expanse of purple flesh, I see his cock straining against his fly. I can't wait another moment to get my hands on it, so I step off the stool and stand in front of him.

"I can't wait to touch you, Sir."

He smiles lazily, his silver gaze burning into me.

Slipping two fingers under his waistband, I slide them back and forth. He's feigning total self-control, but he just sucked in a gasp of air. I'm getting to him.

He's been such a master at playing my body, it's hard to remember there are no women on his planet. For a moment I imagine what it must be like for him—the first time with a woman you've been intimate with for days. A woman you've fantasized about for years. Someone you've flown halfway across the universe to find.

I may hate him, but I want this to be good for him. In nine days I'll be gone, and he'll be womanless. I want to leave him with memories of our time together. I won't even have that.

Snugging my fingers under his waistband, I struggle downward to grasp him in my fist. He's hard as steel with skin as soft as velvet. My fingers explore every inch of him. And there are many inches to explore.

"Fuck," explodes from my lips. It's just overwhelming to have this much masculine power in my hand. "Sorry, Sir."

He doesn't respond, so I continue my research. My fingertips trace along his length as I mentally catalog the ridges and veins. I don't want to wait a moment more, so I unfasten his pants and slide them down, bending my knees as I pull them to the floor.

I squat at his feet, my pussy pulsing in desire as I look up at the sheer size of him—and the sheer length of his cock.

I remember that old saying about trying not to think about a blue elephant, and then the only thing you can think about is a blue elephant. Well, at this moment the only thought pulsing through my brain is that I want him in my mouth so bad I can't stand it. I wonder what the punishment would be if I disobey the one rule he laid out for me.

Pushing that thought aside, I get back to the task at hand— learning Sir.

Grasping his ankles, I brush up his legs memorizing his rounded calves and the tender indents at the back of his knees. He inhales sharply when my thumbs almost reach his balls, then retrace their path down his legs again.

His cock is close to my face and I can see it pulsing, straining to touch me.

Using my nails, I slide up again and see that his attention is more keenly focused on me. On another pass up and down I put even more bite into my touch and receive affirmation that he's enthralled when he presses his lips together more firmly.

After sliding my fingers through my outer lips, I use my slickness to paint up his inner thighs.

"Victoria," he hisses.

"Yes, Sir?" I ask innocently

I'm not surprised he has nothing more to say.

Bending even farther, almost in the apology posture, I ready myself for my next exploration. I pause and pay attention to my arousal. I'm tired of wondering why this position turns me on. It just does.

Turning my head, I nip his inner ankle, then continue up his warm, purple skin. I nip and bite and grab tiny hunks of his skin and toss my head. Moving behind him, I lick the back of his knee and he flinches in surprise. Alternating between his two legs, I nip and lick and scrape the delicate skin there. I think I discovered a new erogenous zone.

Working my way higher, my face is close to his balls when I ask, "Sir, may I touch you here?"

"Where?"

"Your balls, Sir."

"Yes."

First, I grasp him there, registering the weight and warmth of them, then I inch higher and flick one with the tip of my tongue. When he doesn't scold me I lave them with the flat of my tongue. I can't stifle the moan that escapes me. The act is so intimate—like a gift given in secret.

"Stand." His commanding voice sends shivers through me, and I hurry to follow his order.

I'm at his side, looking up into those blazing silver eyes, waiting for his next command. Bending, he grabs my jaw on either side and presses his tongue into my mouth. He mounts an invasion, exploring every inch of me. When I'm breathless and responsive, he snakes a hand between my legs and penetrates me with his fingers.

"Mine."

"Yes, Sir."

"Say it."

"I'm yours, Sir."

He lifts me up and carries me into the shower. This is not quite where I imagined my explorations would end, but he's in charge.

"Make me come."

"Yes, Sir."

I explore the length of him again, this time without the constraints of his pants. When I feel the bead of liquid on the head of his cock, I can't stifle my aroused moan. I circle his tip with the flat of one palm—his hips buck in response.

I know the exact position I want him in, but don't want to overstep.

"Wall, Sir?" I whisper.

He hesitates a moment, then faces the back metal wall of the shower and puts his hands above his head as he leans on it. Every muscle in his back stands out in stark contrast even in the dim light.

"So sexy, Sir."

My palms skim over his skin from flanks to shoulders, then lodge on his cock. I press my front to his back—my nipples caress his skin. One hand grasps his cock while the other holds the heavy weight of his sac. As I stroke him, his hips begin a rhythm that makes my core clench.

His right hand leaves the wall and surrounds my own. He squeezes me around him hard and quickens the rhythm, then releases, his lavender come splattering against the wall.

"Wait for me in bed in the Present position."

I step out of the shower wondering what I did wrong, why he wants to be alone, why he's sending me away.

"That was… amazing, *zara*," he calls to me.

I lie in bed and arrange myself in the perfect position. My thighs are slick and my clit flutters with need.

Voxx enters the room toweling his hair. My attention flies from admiring his perfect body to noticing I've never seen his face so relaxed.

Voxx

"Don't move," I say as I lie on my side next to her. "You did well, Victoria. You're going to be an excellent lover and an excellent mate. Although maybe not an excellent cook."

Her happy smile evaporates. I don't know whether it was the mention of being a mate, or my gentle reproach about her cooking, but I broke the mood.

Gods, she exceeded expectations. She's naturally sensual.

"You've been busy today. Would you like me to coax one more release from you before we review today's lesson?"

"Is the sky blue?"

"No, it's purple why do you ask?"

This she finds uproariously funny.

"Is the sky blue is a rhetorical answer that always means yes because on Earth the sky is blue," she explains as if she's talking to a child.

"No more talking."

I lodge my knees between her thighs and stroke her from head to toe. Well, not exactly stroking. I stay a quarter inch from her skin. She can feel my heat, as I feel hers. I follow every hill and valley closely, but never touch her skin.

Within a minute, she's biting her bottom lip and squirming with need.

"You have ten minutes to come. I'm not going to touch you, *zara*. You're going to think yourself into an orgasm. If you haven't come in ten minutes, I'll stop. If you're a very good girl, I'll fill you up when you're coming.

"No talking. Nod your head if you understand the rules."

She nods and strains upward to receive my touch.

"I'll stop the game if you lean into my touch. Lie perfectly still."

She settles back into the mattress. By the tight expression on her face, she's desperate for my fingers on her skin.

My hands roam from the soles of her feet to the top of her head, but they dawdle at her face, throat, breasts, and the 'v' between her legs. She's moaning now, little mewling noises that sound desperate and make my cock hard. I'm a born Zinn male, I come by this rightfully.

"You only have two minutes left before I stop," I warn sternly.

Within seconds, her hips buck, a sign she's close to release. Taking pity on her, I lean next to her ear and help.

"You're glistening and wet for me. You're so open to me. Imagine my tongue sliding through your folds, finding the well from which all your delicious fluid springs."

She bucks again and is obviously fighting the urge to move.

"I'm a good Sir. Let me help." I dip my head between her legs and blow on her wet channel, then her little button.

"Mmm," she moans but doesn't say a word.

"Good girl," I whisper in her ear. "In thirty seconds. I'm going to tell you to come. When I do, you'll say 'Master' and your release will roll through you like thunder. Nod if you understand the order."

She nods.

"Come."

"Master."

The orgasm blasts her like a tidal wave. I shove three fingers in and pound into her, making certain to touch her bud on every thrust. She throws her arms around my neck and screams her release as it goes on for long moments. Her nails bite into my back—I love their sharp sting.

When all her aftershocks cease, I snuggle next to her, pressing her back to my front. I don't remove my fingers from her channel.

It takes her long moments for her to drift back to reality.

"How was that even possible?" she asks.

"I've heard it said that the mind is the body's largest erogenous zone."

Victoria

I called him Master. What's even more disgusting than that? I know that's what pushed me into that cataclysmic orgasm. How can I loathe myself and feel so fantastic at the same time? I have no idea.

"There's something I need to tell you. Turn around."

I don't like his words—or his tone. Something's barreling at me, I can tell. He's the only person in my world right now who can reassure me or keep me safe, and he's about to deliver bad news.

"I imagine you've wondered why we're at the end of our fifth day and I haven't penetrated you."

Well, yeah. It's like the elephant in the room, but I'm not going to cop to it. It's one of those awful questions that have no correct answer.

He's still waiting, so I make a vague, noncommittal noise and hope he'll read into it whatever he wants.

"Have you, Victoria?"

"Yes, Sir."

"Although it's not in the Interstellar Compact, every book I consulted urges that no penetration occur during the first five days of the Quest. They believe it helps make the ultimate couple-bond stronger. I have abided by that age-old wisdom. Tomorrow, as you well know, is Day Six. I wanted to give you fair warning."

"Yes, Sir."

"From what I've read, this may increase our level of intimacy and draw you more closely to me. I didn't want you to be confused about any feelings you're developing for me."

I'm not developing feelings for you, I tell him in my head. *I've developed lust. And after today who would blame me? But attraction? Real feelings? Don't kid yourself.* What I say out loud is, "Yes, Sir."

"Tomorrow I will lift my self-imposed restrictions. You've asked several times—no, begged if I recall—for me to 'fuck' you. Tomorrow I will."

"Yes, Sir."

"Do you have questions?"

"Nope. That about covers it."

"You pleased me today, *zara*, in many ways. You embraced your desires, or at least you acknowledged them. That takes courage. You explored me in inventive and pleasurable ways. And you called me 'Master' which makes me happy.

"I know I tricked you into saying it, manipulated you. We both know I'm not your Master—yet. But even if you choose poorly on Choosing Day, I'll have that. Good night."

He turns me over so we're spooning again and kisses my head. He curls two fingers into me which calms and soothes me even though I should hate it and push him away.

We're one third through the Quest, and I'm repelled and attracted to him in equal measures. I have nine days to go and it sounds like what happens tomorrow might throw gasoline on the fire of my libido.

I think about how much I hate him at the same time I reach down to press his fingers farther into me.

I'm like a leaf on the wind, not knowing where I'm going, at the mercy of outside forces. But I know one thing with certainty, ten days from now I'll be sleeping in my own bed on planet Earth.

The End

Dear Reader:

I hope you enjoyed Book One in Voxx and Victoria's trilogy. There's so much more to their story. The sexy continuation of Voxx, Book Two and Voxx, Book Three are ready and waiting for you.

Scroll down to read the beginning of the next book, Voxx Book Two.

I wrote an epilogue that will singe your panties (seriously sexy with a little humor thrown in for fun). **This exclusive epilogue is a full novelette and is yours FREE** just for signing up for my newsletter. You can't get it anywhere but through my newsletter. You'll also get all the latest scoop on cover reveals, book previews, and cool giveaways. Sign up for my newsletter here.

"Pretty Please" Request for Reviews:

Remember, leaving reviews on Amazon, Goodreads, and Bookbub can make a huge difference for authors. I'm sure you read reviews before you decide what books to purchase. Your review can help people new to the Mastered by the

Zinn universe decide to take the plunge and check out this amazing new world.

I love hearing from my readers on Facebook, or drop me a line at alanakhanauthor@gmail.com

Hugs,
Alana

Sneak Peak Voxx: Book Two in the Mastered by the Zinn Alien Abduction Romance Series

Present Day
In Space Aboard the two-person vessel the *Drayant*

Day Six

Victoria

I wake in Voxx's warm embrace; he's hot as a furnace. I'm on my side, being spooned from behind, his cock nudging the small of my back.

The last five days have been a revelation. He stole a nerdy law student from her bed and introduced me to levels of sexual passion I'd never even dreamed of—and he hasn't even penetrated me with that gorgeous purple cock of his.

I resisted my own desires for days, but I've come to realize that calling him Sir and following his orders is a huge turn-on for me. My body loves his dominance, and I'm not going to fight it anymore. For the next nine days, I'll try anything he initiates. All I have to do is say "red" and he'll stop.

It's a relief to allow myself to enjoy what he does to my body, knowing that in less than two weeks I'll be back in my bed in Des Moines having totally forgotten about the big, purple asshole from Zinn.

"I want to teach you a new position, Victoria. Ass."

Shit, I didn't even know he was awake. This is the first thing he thinks of the moment he's awake?

"Yes, Sir."

He sits up, plumping the pillows and leaning against them on the headboard. After spreading his legs wide, he says, "Face away from me. Get on all fours between my legs."

As soon as I comply, he adds, "Forehead on the mattress. Good girl."

My ass in all its glory is inches from his face. Stroking the globes of my tush with his palm, he says, "You know what today is?"

"No, Sir."

"Today is the day you feel me inside you."

"Yes, Sir."

"Do you like this position?" His middle finger slides through my folds and plunges inside. "You're already wet for me."

"Yes, Sir." Yesterday I gave up my resistance. It was futile. Yeah, I know, Borg reference. I'm not coy. I'm not a virgin. If I'm turned on, it's no use trying to hide it. I reach back to meet him each time his finger penetrates me.

A second finger joins the first and I could come with just the slightest pressure on my clit.

"Look at the screen, Victoria."

I lift my head to the one-foot by two-foot screen on the wall in front of me. It reads "5:59:56."

"We're going to play a little game today. As you know, I've given you release dozens of times since you joined me on this ship. You've relieved me once, last night when you stroked me in the shower. Today, we'll turn the tables. You'll relieve me many times today. You'll receive your relief when that clock gets to zero."

"Six Earth hours, Sir?"

"Yes. I read about this on your Earth internet. It's called edging."

Being in close proximity to Voxx, with him knowing everything there is to know about my sexual response cycle and I can't come for six hours? I'm already an inch away from orgasm, how can I keep my traitorous body in check all day?

"Any questions about the rules?"

"No, Sir."

"Make me *chernoy* for breakfast." He pulls out of me, swats my ass, and leaves the bed.

"Yes, Sir."

I wash quickly in the small adjoining bathroom, then trot into the kitchen. Since I'm not allowed to wear clothes I don't have a big morning ritual sucking up any of my precious time.

Of course, he had to order me to cook *chernoy*. It was my botched attempt to cook it yesterday that precipitated my personal epiphany that I have submissive tendencies. Well, it wasn't exactly my botched attempt at cooking that triggered my epiphany. It was my body's response to his punishment for a job poorly done.

After I assemble all the ingredients on the counter, he comes up behind me, grasps both my shoulders, and leans, his lips next to my ear. I melt at just this calming touch. "Do you remember the rules?"

"I remember how to cook it for you, Sir."

"I would hope so after yesterday's disaster. But I'm asking if you recall what you should be thinking about while you prepare food for your Sir."

"Yes, Sir."

"Edify me."

"Every act I perform should be in service of our bond, Sir. I should think about your pleasure when I do even the most mundane task."

"Very good, Victoria." He slides my long, chestnut hair over my shoulder and kisses up my neck. "You woke up in a very good mood this morning. A different male might regret the choice of tormenting you all day."

He swats my ass again, then saunters to the captain's chair ten feet away.

I've never been a rule breaker. This fact entered into the equation yesterday when I determined I was a submissive. I like having parameters. I enjoy striving to color within the lines. I don't bother questioning myself as I prepare his meal with care, following the instructions perfectly.

When the *chernoy* is cooked, I spoon it into a bowl, mindful to keep milky splatters off the wide rim.

"Where would you like me to serve it to you, Sir?"

"Here, come kneel in front of me."

I do just as he says, kneeling directly in front of his captain's chair, then handing him the bowl. I wait impatiently for him to taste it. Gone are all worries of finals and time crunches and paying bills. Right this moment, my biggest concern is whether Voxx from Zinn will approve of how I cooked his *chernoy*.

I don't want an instant replay of yesterday when he was disappointed in the way I prepared his breakfast.

Actually the most disturbing thing about that episode wasn't the objectification and threat of punishment. The most humbling part was the way my core lubricated at his treatment.

"Very good, Victoria," he announces as he nods his head. "Not only did you cook this exactly as I asked you to, but you served it to me in a pleasing fashion. This is how I wish you would service all of my requests. I will reward you by removing one hour from your restriction."

I'm afraid to glance at the clock. I think taking my eyes from him might break a rule.

"Come closer." He pats his knee and I scoot toward him. "Here." He spoons me a bite.

"Thank you, Sir."

He takes turns feeding himself and me. I allow myself to enjoy eating out of his hand. I try to banish my self-loathing at relishing in his attention.

"You seem more serene today, Victoria. Is that correct?"

"Yes, Sir."

"Why is that?"

"I've quit fighting my own impulses, Sir. I've decided to embrace my desires, one of which is to please you."

"Excellent. Right now it will please me for you to clean the galley. Then it will please me to re-introduce you to the *krannock*."

I cock an eyebrow in question but am afraid to ask.

"The machine taking up half the galley. You called it 'sex furniture' I believe. It offers infinite positions, both for pleasure and pain."

Shit. That's the machine I was tied to when I woke up on board this ship. I'd hoped it was a 'one and done' sort of thing. The look on Attila the Zinn's handsome face tells me there's no arguing with his idea. Okay, I take a deep breath, *krannock* it is.

As I finish cleaning, I glance at one of the screens posted all over the ship. 3:12:33. I'm in close quarters with a sex god who knows every spot on my body—both inside and out— that turns me on, and I have over three hours before I can come. I try to convince myself this will be child's play.

"Before I put you on the *krannock*, here's another position for today. Inspect."

"Yes, Sir."

My eyes widen in fright when I see the black riding crop in his hand. He points toward the *krannock* with it.

"Stand as tall as possible with your hands behind your neck, legs wide, eyes on me. "

"Yes, Sir." I comply.

"Legs wider. Breasts out to please your Sir."

"Yes, Sir."

In the past, I was only focused on how much I hated the big, purple asshole and how much I resented being here. Today, I allow my mind to settle into an appreciation of my position.

I'm on display for Voxx. My most private spaces are open to the air, my breasts are thrust out, and the best part of the equation is the look of pure appreciation in his eyes. This isn't half as bad as I made it out to be.

Out of my peripheral vision, I snag a glimpse of the wall of torture as I call it. There are whips and other sex toys that scare the crap out of me. I may have decided to go with the flow until choosing day, but I'm still Victoria, and I still hate pain.

Voxx is behind me, stroking me with the leather riding crop from inner ankle to outer lips to the other ankle. He's never hurt me with the crop, and I let myself get lulled into relaxation by its slow slide on my skin.

"Open your mouth."

"Yes, Sir."

"Hold this." He puts the crop in my mouth and I clamp my teeth around it. I imagine what I must look like—in my mind's eye, despite my submissive posture, I look kind of sexy.

Stepping closer, his hands cup the globes of my ass. Two fingers dip between my legs and spread my liquid to my clit, then plunge into me. His other hand cups me from in front, two fingers plucking my clit. I bend my knees to garner more pressure from both hands.

"This displeases me, Victoria. I don't want you to forget who is in charge. The Inspect pose is for my enjoyment, not yours. I'm adding a half-hour punishment."

"Yes, Sir."

He's still behind me, so my eyes flick up to the screen in front of me to see 3:25:54.

"In the future, I want you to thank me for every punishment. I only do these things to help you be a better submissive."

"Yes, Sir. Thank you, Sir." *Don't fight this*, I urge myself. *Pretend this is a game.* As much as my mind rebels at this and wants to hate him, my body is on fire for him right now.

"You may put your hands at your sides and walk to the wall. I'd like you to inspect the dildos carefully. Pick one that will provide pleasure to your ass."

"Yes, Sir."

Pleasure. That's a great operative word. Although I thought I'd hate it, I loved his fingers back there. I find a dildo that is a close approximation to the width of his two fingers, it's blue.

"Approach me, kneel, and hand it to me. Tell me what you want me to do with it."

I kneel at his feet and gaze up at his piercing silver eyes as he towers over me. "I'd like you to penetrate me with this, Sir."

"Be more graphic."

"I want you to fuck me in the ass with this, Sir. And make me come." I add as an afterthought, "If it pleases you, Sir." I don't want to forget he's the dominant.

"I believe you forgot who's in charge again, Victoria. When you come is a decision only I make. I'm adding thirty minutes. No, make that ninety minutes."

Shit.

"Thank you for teaching me my place, Sir." *It's just a game, Victoria*—my new mantra.

"There's a way to remove your punishment."

He's baiting me. I have a feeling what he's going to say next is actually the point of this whole exercise.

"I will remove all ninety minutes if you go to the wall and pick out a dildo that will challenge you. After all," he pauses until I lift my eyes to him, "you'll need to take this. Soon." He grabs his hard purple cock in his large purple hand.

Well, yeah, the elephant in the room. That humongous thing's about to go into a lot of places that aren't quite ready to be invaded.

"Yes, Sir. Very generous of you, Sir."

As I stroll to the wall of torture, I notice a lusty zing of anticipation reverberating through my body. Why, I wonder, do I keep repeating that I don't do pain if the thought of this makes me wet?

It's hard to miss the dildo I should pick—it's purple and about as big as Voxx's cock. I pick the one next to it, it's chartreuse and a bit smaller than my Sir's. Did I really just do that? Did I really call him 'my Sir' in my own head? I thought this was all a game. I refuse to buy into all his bullshit. Evidently some part of my mind didn't get the memo.

I walk back to him, kneel at his feet and lift it up toward him. "I want you to fuck me with this, Sir. It's just a bit smaller than y ou are and the first time I'm breached with something that big, I want it to be your beautiful cock. Sir."

Not only did I say that, I said it without irony—or paradox. And dear God, I meant it.

Click here to buy Voxx Book Two

Acknowledgements:

Hugs to everyone on my Alpha, Beta, and ARC teams. You challenge me to up my game! Special thanks to C.O.,J.M., R.C., L.L., K.H., K.F., F.T., as well as to Erin, my P.A. (you'll be missed) and my beloved daughter.

Copyright

Voxx: Book One in the Mastered by the Zinn Alien Abduction Romance Series by Alana Khan

P.O. Box 18393, Golden, CO 80402

www.alanakhan.com

Cover by Elle Arden

Printed in Great Britain
by Amazon

38748245R00111